ATHENA

ATHENA
DARK EMPRESS

ROMMELL C. LEWIS

Authored and published by Rommell C. Lewis

ISBN-13: 9780692048672
ISBN-10: 0692048677

AUTHOR'S NOTE

This book is intended for a mature adult audience. This book is not intended for children, teens, young adults, or anyone who cannot separate fantasy from reality. This book contains offensive scenes and violence, including *sex, murder, killing, swearing, abuse, rape, racism, torture, misogyny, sado-masochism*, and *religious blasphemy*. If you are an adult who is offended by such material, you are highly advised not to purchase or read this book.

This book is a work of fiction, and any relation to any real person, living, dead, or otherwise; locales; or real situations is purely coincidental. Keep this book out of the reach of young children and minors. The author will not be held responsible for any injury, theft, loss of property, damage, or death that results from you or anyone else reading this book. This book is for entertainment purposes only.

To no one.

The Price of Greed

ALPHA CAMP, PLANET GURON-1PC—880 CD

"Now, honey, how do you expect me to get any work done, with you sucking on my dick?" asked Matthew Graesen, looking at the top of Caroline's brunette head. He relished the sounds of her wet mouth polishing his knob. The thirty-nine-Earth-years-old mining supervisor patted his wife's glistening shoulders and leaned back with a cigarette in his mouth. He felt her hands caress his bare and hairy chest. He was about to pop in the woman's mouth, when a worker flung open the tent.

"Stupid bastard. How about ya fucking knock next time!" said Matt.

Caroline yelped and wiped her lips. She stood up and stormed out.

"See what you done? Goddamn it. I'm taking this out of your pay."

The sixty-day mining operation and the lackeys who came with it were siphoning his last nerve. Five more days—or five minutes, if he chose to blow his head off. But where's the fun in that? Just a little longer, and he'd be fifty grand richer.

"You just gonna stand there like a fucking retard or open your mouth and squabble?"

The girl, no older than nineteen Earth years, said, "We found something, but…"

"But what?" Matt's long brown hair was wet against his back. "Spit it out, or quit wasting my time."

Matt pored over the girl's slender body, and his member remained erect at her moist cleavage, womanly scent, and blond hair tucked underneath her yellow mining helmet.

"We think you should come take a look."

Matt picked up his semiautomatic rifle and fastened his helmet on his head. He shoved past the hot but nervous wreck and made for the rover that was situated across the camp. He'd been digging and chipping away at rocks for much too long. When he first started, his supervisor would've socked him cold just for leaving the site without permission. Nowadays, he saw the miners as nothing more than a bunch of faggots, liberal college kids, or lazy coloreds demanding a handout. *You don't dig, you don't eat. You don't dig, you don't sleep. You don't dig, you go home empty handed*—words that used to have meaning in his day. He cursed at the thought of Sentinel's regulations, which were tighter than a virgin's cunt. Tell a nail-polished boy he had to work past dinner, and he'd be in the Citadel chipping shit off the toilets.

Matt leaped over the driver's door and into the split compartment. He stashed the rifle in the center weapon rack. The girl opened the door to the passenger side and got in. And off they went to the mine, ten miles away.

Helios—the solar system's mother star—baked Matt's back as he eyed the mountainous terrain ahead of them. He swiped a used towel across his forehead. Things would only get hotter and stickier as the forty-eight-hour day engulfed this side of the planet. He found extreme comfort when Helios retired itself, giving way to twenty-four hours of night. Despite the odd weather pattern, Sentinel had ordered expeditions to work nonstop mining syncorium—an element used to power Athena. What boggled his mind was why Sentinel had chosen this particular area for the deployment. His team had found nothing but scraps. Barely enough to run a neighborhood for two months. This was Guron-1PC's southern hemisphere. The north was rich in syncorium deposits. But who gave a shit? At the end of the day, the pay was all that mattered.

"What's your name?" he asked the blonde.

"Terry," she said.

"Terry, huh?" The rover hit a road that'd been flattened for easy access from the camp to the mine. "Why haven't I seen you around? Kinda young for work like this. Got something to prove?" He sped up and went over a hill. Just a little way north lay the mountainside, with its mouth wide open. The team had created the opening, as there had been no visible entrance.

The rover began kicking up dust.

"Nah, nah. That's not it. How about college? You look like the type."

"What type is that, sir?"

Approximately three hundred yards ahead were additional rovers off to the side of the road.

"You know. The…the drunk parties. All-nighters. Blowing the bouncer to get in the club. That type—am I right?"

She smiled and said, "You got it. I'm a cum-gargling, drunken slut. The only way a girl can make it in this world." She sighed.

"Hot damn! I knew it. Damn, I knew it."

"My undergrad's in religious studies. I graduate next summer. After that, no more fun for, like, the rest of my life. Maybe I should switch majors—you know. I want to be something exciting, like a legionnaire. The ones who give tickets and arrest people."

"Nah, you don't want to do that. Now, the collegium is definitely in need of a girl like you." Matt was a former priest who held a doctorate in religious studies. He had been fired from his professor position at the Centurion Academy for having sex with an unconscious eighteen-Earth-year-old at a frat party. The collegium pontificum stripped his priesthood but went easy and banished him to the mines. It was the least they could do, considering he had evidence that the pontifex maximus at the time had beaten a new male student to death. A slip and fall, they'd ruled it.

Terry's type was his weakness—young, blond, hot, and vulnerable. He had had a good trading system going until the night his big head became too inebriated to prevent the little one from doing all the talking. *Oh well, such is life.*

There was some way to go before they made it to the cave. He was sure she could use the money, and who was she to tell him no? His camp, his rules. And rule number one: keep your mouth shut.

Matt said to Terry, "You gotta work hard out here. Earn your cut."

"True."

"'Cause those books ain't gonna pay for themselves."

"You got that right!" She snorted while laughing.

"I got a close associate who owes me some favors. Now, I know a pretty piece like you *has* to be looking to get into the college. One day become the first female ponti, and all that shit. Trust me; you won't be the only one. I've seen the most qualified come crying out the ponti's office. They only let a select few women in. Best way is to have a connection. To know someone on the inside."

"How did you know that's what I wanted? Well, my parents, at least."

"Like I said, I know your type. How about this? I give you ample time to study and a few extra niceties, and I'll talk to my associate, if you...show me a little generosity every now and then. You know what I'm saying."

"Do you want me to suck your cock?"

"And bold, are we. I like that. Thought you'd never ask."

"You're such a kidder. Why didn't you just say so? You're clean—sorta. My goal is to blow two hundred guys before graduation. It's a contest we got going. I'm up to one fifteen. Can you believe my best friend, who's in the same program, is at one forty already? Since we're on summer break, I was thinking of checking with some of the guys on site, but they're so old and funky. Like total rejects. Like gross. Anyways, if I make it to the college, who knows when I'll get some? Probably never. But...your wife, sir?"

"Let me tell you, she's no angel. Believe you me."

"They never are. One sixteen, here I come. Or here you cum? Don't laugh. Bad joke." Terry unzipped Matt's shorts and leaned over to swallow his meatsicle. He slowed the rover to enjoy the moment. She was even better than he had fantasized. Reminded him of one of his A+ students. Her moist tongue bathed his cock's underside. He slumped down a tad, feeling and hearing Terry choke herself on his dick. He removed her helmet and watched the sweat run off her neck.

"Fuck. Uh yeah," he moaned. "Show me what you're made of. That's right. Suck it."

She popped her head up, looked out the windshield, and began stroking him at an even pace.

"You gonna take care of me, daddy?" she asked, jerking his dick. "You gotta promise."

"Yeah, sure. That's it. Uh, shit!" He was sensitive enough from Caroline's blow job to drown Terry's soft white hands in loads of jizz—something he had reserved for his wife's mouth.

Terry brought her slimy knuckles to her lips and cleaned them. She helped him zip up as the rover came to a stop.

"Put this back on, kid," he said, forcing the helmet down on her head.

"Sir!" called a middle-aged miner running from the cave.

"Yeah. You found something," he said. Matt armed his rifle and stepped out of the rover. "What is it, and where is it?"

Terry attempted to tag along behind Matt.

"Shoo. They don't pay us to stand around," said Matt.

Terry frowned at him, huffed, and said, "Asshole," under her breath but loud enough for him to hear it.

The unnamed miner mimicked Terry's action, and Matt followed. Two freight pilots looked on as he rushed to investigate the commotion.

Outside was tough, but this was suffocating. He wheezed, pushing farther and farther forward. Lighting his way were glow sticks tossed into random spaces on the ground. Matt's searing skin was cooled by a tunneling wind. Thirty days ago had been the first time he'd passed through the cave's entrance. He typically tiptoed around back to catch the bastards smoking and joking. However, his instinct and the look on the unnamed miner's face told him this was no laughing matter. For the first time in a long while, his heart rate increased, and internal temperature plummeted.

A few meters ahead was a green light that outlined a handful of workers who were standing near a blasted opening. Terry stopped next to the miners, and they all moved aside for Matt. He slung his rifle over a shoulder and pressed through the hole. He shielded his eyes against the light with a palm. He stopped and stared at a glowing object that was embedded into hard rock.

"Don't touch it!" warned a miner. "Poor fella earlier burned his hand off."

Matt retracted his fingers. He watched currents zigzag through the object's visible parts.

"What do you think it is?" asked Terry from behind.

"A mansion on a private island and all the pussy I can eat." He turned and yelled back. "Will someone get a goddamn drill on this thing!"

"Right away, sir!"

Several minutes later, a crew labored at the space around the unknown device.

"Who do you think made it?" asked Terry.

"Stop asking me a buncha dumbass questions and go get my transmitter."

Terry complied without argument.

The crew made good progress, and rocks piled up. The object became extremely luminescent, exposing more of its alien structure. At this point, the girl's inquiry became more relevant.

"What the hell is this?" he said under his breath.

A few extra pounds of elbow grease knocked the object loose to the floor. The perfect sphere, about the size of a bowling ball, pulsated, and its heat brushed his cheeks. Terry returned with the transmitter.

He snatched it from her and radioed the transporter in high orbit. "Tango-Ten, Tango-Ten, this is Charlie-Seven."

"Reading you loud and clear. Go with your message," they came back.

"Yeah. My men have located some kinda weird glowing contraption here at the site. Not sure what to make of it. We're gonna prep it for evacuation so you guys can take a look at it."

A long pause. "That won't be necessary. Mark it, and depart the site."

Just what he'd expected. The assholes at Sentinel wanted to cash in first. "You sure we should leave this thing unguarded?" he asked.

Another transmission break. "That won't be necessary, Charlie-Seven. Your orders are to tag and retreat."

And then a wild idea crossed his mind. Undetected, Matt armed a dynabomb sticking out of a miner's rucksack and thieved a pair of extra-thick work gloves.

"Well, you heard them. Let's scram," Matt told his crew.

"Sixty seconds," read the bomb's digital face. He eased off the pack to allow them some distance. He nestled his hands into the gloves and slowed down even more. Terry looked back but kept moving forward. The gap widened considerably as they conversed, unaware of their fate. Despite his murderous intentions, something told him their sacrifice was necessary, that there were bigger things at stake than his own greed.

The team neared the entrance, and the bomb's timer sounded. The miner dropped the sack and said, "Sh—"

Boooom! Matt sprinted back to the sphere as heavy boulders dropped behind him. Their screams were useless. He only hoped they'd die quickly. But that was wishful thinking. He reckoned that Terry's legs would lay crushed for hours—or at worst, days—as she starved and bled a slow death.

As Matt reached the sphere, an eruption sounded, and layers of debris toppled him.

"No!" he cried, diving for *his* discovery. The ground under the sphere caved in, and it sank below. Rock fell on the space and covered the hole.

ENDGAME

INFERNO, PLANET
ATHENA—HEPHAESTUS 27, 899 CD

Emperor Thaddeus Augustus Claudius looked out the shuttle's window at the gathering in the city square. In the crowd's center, a black-armored and black-helmeted legionnaire stomped a peasant in the back of his leg, forcing him to kneel. The soldier yanked the man's hair back, making him watch the shuttle land.

The door opened, and Thaddeus exited, followed by six armed legionnaires. Loose lips tightened as the solar system's leader parted his people. His bald head roasted under Helios in the planet's hottest and poorest region. The city was home to the worst Athena had to offer: murderers, thieves, and those on the run.

A ranking legionnaire rendered a salute.

The prisoner spat at the cloaked leader's battle-scarred face and eye patch. The drool ran down onto his black muscle cuirass.

"So this is the one," said Thaddeus. The sweaty man's rags were torn from head to toe. "The one who decided these people would fare better with greener pastures?"

Sentinel had charged the man with an executable ordinance violation. He'd bioengineered fruit and vegetable seeds that could withstand Inferno's harsh atmosphere. Farming for any commoner was illegal.

"Why award laziness?" asked Thaddeus. "They contribute absolutely nothing to our economy. They're parasites, feeding off the backs of hardworking people."

He raised an arm, and an automatic weapon extracted from his gauntlet. "But you. You were so much more." The emperor blew the man's head off at point-blank range. He regarded the legionnaires pouring fuel on a nearby greenhouse. A rupture occurred, and the greenhouse lit aflame.

"The next time…I'll kill all of you," warned Thaddeus, following the legionnaires. His weapon retracted.

The crowd began to disperse.

A six-wheeled, black-camouflaged rover rolled to a stop. The side door lifted, and his second-in-command stepped out. The wind created a light dusting that blew Phylyx Kronos's pitch-white, long blond hair and black cloak as Emperor Claudius approached and returned a salute. The lead Serpent's torso was protected by a matching cuirass that bore an engraved golden serpent in its chest. The emperor looked over his armament—a drop holster and side arm, absent his honorary Serpent Blade.

"I must say that I'm impressed," said Thaddeus.

"Well received, My Emperor," said Kronos. "Unsanctioned scientific experimentation is a dangerous practice."

"Walk with me."

Two flanks of legionnaires protected Thaddeus and Kronos as they traveled the dusty city street.

"Also, I must advise you that I've grown impatient," Thaddeus said. "*They've* grown impatient."

Kronos said, "I assure you that we won't cease until it's found."

"My greatest concern is a matter of their true intentions. We must exercise due caution."

"A bargaining chip, I take it," said Kronos.

"We both know that *these things* are not bound by any honor code. To negotiate is to willingly serve our heads on a silver platter." Claudius looked to the sky. "Almost eighteen hundred years since colonization, and nothing has changed. They're a cosmic mistake that infects every world it touches."

Thaddeus witnessed a young female sweeping dust from a shipping container that served as her home. Her golden hair flowed in the wind. He assumed her rags were hand-me-downs going back multiple generations. Of course, she shat children from different fathers, which she could barely afford to feed and clothe. He knew that she labored on her knees to earn a few extra coins to pay off taxes or a local debt.

Thaddeus spoke on. "The empire has reached a crossroad. And by the will of the gods, I refuse to fiddle while it burns." He stopped and took a knee. He dug his iron fist into the ground and lifted a claw full of sand and funneled it. "This is all that will be left if we do not act now." He rose and looked back at the row of containers and clotheslines hanging from them.

Kronos said, "There is an option to rid of us of our troubles."

Thaddeus said, "The Omega."

"My thoughts exactly."

"It should come as no surprise to you that I've given it careful consideration."

"The elders would prove tough to convince."

The emperor was prepared to do what the other emperors would not. "We've answered humankind's greatest question. Now it is time we bury it."

Kronos walked with his hands behind his cloak and eyes to the ground. "We must remember that intelligence breeds a violent war at the top of the food chain. If the tables were turned, would they have shown the same compassion or exterminated us on sight?"

The men stopped walking.

"This ends now," said Thaddeus.

Kronos's digital SpecNav chirped. He rotated his gauntlet to its underside and pressed a button.

The Sentinel battle station, a four-hundred-mile-long spaceship orbiting the planet, came online. "My Lord, we've detected an unusual cloud formation over the western hemisphere." Kronos maximized a real-time holographic image of Planet Athena. He zoomed in to the area that was home to the mountainous megacity Utopis. "The weather patterns inside the clouds are off the charts. Our satellites are showing a temperature range of two hundred degrees and climbing." A dark volcanic mass expanded from zero point and covered portions of the terrain.

"Noted," said Kronos before the hologram funneled into his SpecNav. Thaddeus watched him send his coordinates. "It appears my assistance is required on station."

"I'll travel to—"

Kronos said, "Perhaps it's best if I had the honor."

The emperor hesitated a brief moment but said, "Very well." It would be Kronos's neck on the line if the elders disapproved of a man other than the anointed emperor speaking before them. Even a lord was shown no mercy. To Kronos's advantage, this unspoken sin was not included in the Decree, a centuries-old document that governed the emperor's actions and served as the basis for all galactic law.

A slanted wing transport began its descent, blowing their capes in scattering sand. The black spacecraft released its circular landing gear, which was attached to two metallic legs.

Thoomp. Tss.

Kronos rendered a salute and turned toward the craft. Three legionnaires escorted the future emperor to the lowering ramp.

Claudius knew he could trust Kronos to speak to the elders on his behalf. Convince them that the planet's twenty-five million inhabitants and the Roman Empire's very existence depended on this monumental decision. He was positive the elders would never approve of his actions. This was only a courtesy.

TO THE VICTOR!

CENAEUS AMPHITHEATER, UTOPIS, PLANET ATHENA—HEPHAESTUS 27, 899 CD

The hypogeum's cement floor shook under Augustine's feet as thousands of voices and stomping feet rocked the amphitheater. The emperor's dark-brunette daughter took a deep breath after witnessing a fallen body block the afternoon sunlight that shone through the grate above her head. Standing on a circular platform that would take her to the arena floor, she squeezed the sword's and shield's handles tight. Drips of blood tapped her white cheeks and nose. A two-man crew cleared the dead, and her face felt warm once more.

"It's party time!" said a familiar voice from behind her. "Uh, excuse us?"

She lowered and shook her head inside the galea and then turned around. What were they doing here? Why now?

"Ain't you some hot shit?" said Meegan Kronos, her best friend and daughter of Lord Kronos. The blonde had recently turned eighteen Earth years old, and today Meegan was celebrating her birthday. As typical of Meegan, vodka seeped from every orifice before a night out. Her equally wasted gang of five were never far off.

Two girls began traveling together throughout the stone room, tickling gladiator biceps and blowing kisses as they passed. The two noble daughters stopped, looked at each other, and said, "Nah." They passed up four additional wounded men, who'd been spared death, and halted at the one closest to Augustine.

Her friends loved to play this sick and twisted game with the condemned. Augustine imagined the unlucky ones silently berating the brunettes with the unholiest of names. In the blink of an eye, they dropped to their knees, with one opening her mouth. The other girl giggled, digging for his flesh stick. She fished his dick out and began fisting him off in her friend's mouth.

"Fucking cock addicts." Meegan laughed. She addressed Augustine. "Aren't you happy to see us? We came to cheer you on."

Today was the last day of the gladiator games. Augustine had entered the blood-spilled contest to show to Athena that nobility bled just as they did. With the emperor on a mission, she had tossed Octavianus, the slave master, a hefty coin to silence him. But the eighty grand he had received only went so far. The theater was packed with inebriated spectators awaiting her entrance.

A monstrous and deep roar opened the bowels of hades. "Cyril! Cyril! Cyril!" they chanted. Cyril, a.k.a. the Bone Grinder. The notorious blacksmith who had kidnapped three high-school girls, raped and skinned them, and then forged their bones into kitchen utensils to devour their organs. His body, sword, and shield were stained with the blood of thirty-nine slaves. *Today, his reign will end*, she thought, smashing her closed fist against the shield.

The grate opened, and the circular platform shifted under her boots.

"Yeah, big daddy. Shoot that nut," said her friend as she was spattered with man juice.

"That's your cue, tiger," said Meegan.

Augustine turned back around, lowered her head, and exhaled. Her long red legionnaire cape swept the dusty floor. Her bronze muscle cuirass squeezed her abdomen and shoulders.

"Watch it, jackass!" said Meegan as someone bumped shoulders with her.

"Your call," said Octavianus, dressed in a traditional red Roman pallium and sandals. "I can say something came up—emergency. Anything along those lines."

She eyed the shiny-bald-headed negro and said, "Pray the gods dull my sword."

He pulled the transmitter from under his cloak and said, "Match is a go. I repeat, match is a go."

"That's my girl! Woo-hoo!" said Meegan.

The six chicks pranced out the hypogeum to catch the elevator to their high seats above the theater.

The platform ascended, and the crowd became rabid. Augustine kept her head down and eyes closed. Seconds later, the platform secured. She opened her eyes to a sea of crazed Athenians. She saw her digital self, bent at the waist with her fist balled up. The "vs." abbreviation separated her and the darkest negro she'd ever seen. His arms were spread, showing off his rock-solid frame. Under his image was the number 39.

Cyril stood about fifty feet away, and his skin appeared slick. He wore no garments, and his python cock nearly dragged in the dirt. The undefeated champion threw his sword and shield to opposite sides. "Come get it, you lil bitch!" he yelled, jerking himself at Augustine. His throat barked the laughter of a thousand demonic hounds.

Augustine followed his move. Her sword and shield hit the amphitheater's dusty tarmac, to the crowd's approval.

"Oh, you den fucked up now, lil girl." Cyril socked an open palm with his fist and turned into a bulldozer at a hundred miles a second.

The teen went spinning airborne, extended her leg, and wrecked the Bone Grinder's jaw. Cyril's body cartwheeled right and ended prone.

The stadium went mad.

The champion pushed up on his knuckles and finally stood to. He came at her once more. Augustine's front jab was blocked by his forearm, and her stomach pushed in. The devastating blow caused her to come off her feet. Two interlinked fists dropped down on her spine midair.

"Arrgh!"

A knee was buried into her lower back, and the crowd booed. Another knee drop. "Boo!"

His eclipsing shadow soon gave way to daylight. She paid no mind to her pulsating muscles and came up. Cyril flexed at the disapproving spectators, who threw trash and shit toward the arena floor.

"She's just a girl!" snorted a male from far away.

"Yeah! Show some respect!"

Augustine sprinted, leaped at Cyril, wrapped her arm around the rear of a prodigious neck, clasped her fingers on her wrist, and drove him into the dirt. She started choking the life out of him, but Cyril powered through and stood with his hand under her thighs.

Wham! A well-executed backdrop. Her ribs seemed to crack under his weight. Panting and spitting, he flipped over on her body and wrapped a jumbo paw around her throat and used the other to smack away her hands. Cyril sniffed her funky BO and raged, "I gets off on da stench of bleeding virgins." He punched the side of her face, caving in the galea, and then clawed it off. The helmet's landing mixed with the crowd's howls. His salty sweat leaked on her lips as his eyes casted toward Tiberius Camerius—the Galactic Gladiator League's wealthy CEO.

Cyril menaced at Augustine through clenched teeth, and then she was able to breathe. He got up and stepped over her body. He'd secured the first pin. Best two out of three.

The crowd's boos became louder. She rolled over, keeping her hands under her chest.

Augustine stood, and he bounded for her with his weapon drawn. The Bone Grinder's sword swung down, and she rolled right.

Clank, clank, clank.

On her final roll, she swooped up her weapons and blocked the assault with her shield.

With all her might, she pushed up, forcing Cyril backward. Augustine gained momentum and warred forth with sword and shield. Her weapon sliced the air above his ducking shoulders. She sidestepped his frontal lunge and forced her sword down against his. A forty-five-degree movement slashed his chest, and she repeated the strike in the opposite direction. Cyril stumbled back, but Augustine refused to let up. She crisscrossed her sword against his skin with no mercy. His arm was severed before his weapon rose. She jumped, double kicked his lacerated chest, and performed a front flip. On the descent, she spread her thighs and landed with her crotch on his stomach. The blade brushed his throat.

One to one.

The amphitheater was on its feet, screaming like fucking banshees.

Cyril's brutish persona could not deny the fear creeping in his eyes. Through his veins and heart. Augustine's senses were driven mad by the sight and smell of his blood and nub. She kept her reserve, yet the animal in her called for his life, overpowering her expected humanity.

The theater quieted, and she eased off to a standing position. She was not her father, who'd slay a citizen in front of his own people.

The Bone Grinder finally got up, breathing heavily, with half a limb. "So...do it."

Augustine's long brunette hair was soaked on her cheeks. The match was an easy win, seeing as Cyril was missing an arm. Unfair, even.

"Finish him!" blurted an unseen woman.

She observed the endless seats of salivating citizens. She reversed and headed for the hypogeum's platform.

Cyril said, "I was stupid to believe you, the noble *whore*, would fight me to the death." He raised his voice. "I guess that's what the people get from a selfish child who was raised by a pompous bitch!"

The Centurion Academy's former discus champion released the sword into a twirl.

The crowd became alive. Cyril's knees hit first. His headless torso went forward onto the theater's dirt floor.

Two, one—the gigantic scoreboard flashed her victory. The amphitheater turned into one mass party.

Having freshly showered, a guarded Augustine waited outside the Cenaeus Amphitheater for her personal rover to arrive.

Boozed gladiator fans wobbled out the main entrance. The toga-wearing lushes heaved on their sandals or into overflowing garbage cans. She saw two boys fight with wooden swords, rehearsing the main event's final scene, causing her to smile a little.

The black rover arrived, and she hopped into the two-seater and sped off.

The win wasn't as joyful as she'd thought. Augustine sighed and rested an elbow out the window, using her knuckles to support her head. She inhaled the mountain air that permeated the warm winds on her face. One year left on Athena, and she had barely lived a day. She'd spent her childhood and early teenage years at the Legionnaire Academy studying strategy and training for combat that never came. In her late teens, she honed her skills at Sentinel's Centurion Academy. Skills that she would only put to use in her dreams. Augustine envied the Serpents who led centurions into alien territory on distant worlds. Slaying wild beasts and discovering new elements, treasures. She scorned the ones like Kronos, who sat on their asses barking mindless orders, having never lifted a sword.

Her studies were nothing but a waste. No emperor's daughter, at her age, was ever thrust into battle. Combat came when they had gray hair or grew bald. By then she would be as senile and short tempered as her father. Her looming execution was sure to snuff out any hope of charging into war. *War? What war?* The last true battle had happened two hundred Earth years ago, in 799 CD, during the Defiance Wars. The pathetic and deserved scratch on her father's face wasn't anything compared to the assassinations Emperor Julianus Floronius Isauricus's order had suffered at the end of his reign. This fear of the people gave her bloodline a rationalization to subdue them at all costs.

The digital speedometer increased its numbers—110, 120, 140 mph. Augustine took her hands off the steering wheel and raised them in the air when the rover climbed a hill.

"Oh yeah!" she said, coming down on all four tires. The palace, in its dark and monumental glory, appeared in the horizon. A reinforced stone wall, approximately twenty miles in circumference and a hundred yards thick, protected its emperor. The palace was a small city in and of itself. High-ranking government employees and contractors raised their families in immaculate residential districts. Children attended the finest schools and studied sciences forbidden to the poor. As a fourth-grader, Augustine was able to understand the theory behind faster-than-light travel, though the human race had yet to master it. Her physical-science projects consisted of building miniature rockets and shooting them toward a planet named Earth. Her fifth-grade biology professor rated her on how accurately she cloned the planet's native species. Far beyond her home was Utopis's shining skyscrapers.

Augustine shifted gears and stepped on it. She switched the dashboard monitor to the rearview camera as she hit a curve on the winding mountain road. A Sentinel squad rover that was parked behind a billboard for a new strip club never budged. But she would have enjoyed the chase if it had.

Moments later, Augustine slowed at the checkpoint and returned the legionnaire's salute. She winked at him before driving off. She drove down a two-lane road and past a diamond water fountain. The palace was pure luxury. Slaves repaved the streets constantly, cleaned the parks and courtyards, and watered two-hundred-yard-long gardens. The people's taste demanded the refined dishes and first-class spirits served in top-notch restaurants and lounges. They elevated their noses when speaking to others who did not live within its confines and wore their education on their sleeves.

I ain't got time for none of that shit, thought Augustine. Her days were numbered. The only thing she wanted to do was bounce her little ass in the club, drink hard liquor, suck juicy dicks, and smoke until her lungs collapsed. For sure she would find her vices in abundance in Utopis, the upper-middle-class city outside the palace. That was where the real party was.

Party? Shit! She's gonna be pissed. She hooked an illegal U-turn at the next traffic light.

▲   ▲   ▲

VETURIA'S NIGHTCLUB, THE PALACE, PLANET ATHENA—HEPHAESTUS 27, 899 CD

Later that evening, Augustine located her friends across the club's floor at Veturia's, a happening spot for twentysome-things. Acidic Tampon, the best-selling thrash metal band, were shredding on stage. Meegan was seated at a leather booth for eight. The devious blonde was the only one who recognized her enter unfashionably late.

Augustine sat Meegan's bagged gift on the glass and squeezed in between her friend and another girl at the booth.

"Bitch, what took you so long?" asked Meegan, with red and glossy eyes and smeared lipstick.

Augustine smiled and motioned a hand to the bag for her to open it.

"An 899 CD LXR? You fucking bought me yesteryear's luxury rover? I can't believe this. You slut," said a stoned Meegan, holding the price tag. The girls laughed.

Augustine didn't join in on the joke and veered her eyes toward the bar. She'd spent all evening tracking down the specific model her friend had asked for just a week ago.

"Come here," said Meegan, and she hugged Augustine. Her friend's hair reminded her of the cinnamon apples that grew in the front yard. Her skin was wet, and her gray shirt stank of cigarettes.

A slave approached the group, bowed, and said, "Good evening, my lady."

She was serious was her first thought upon seeing the bare-chested negro, who wore only a bow tie and black undies.

"Evening to you too, my good sir," she replied.

"Sir?" Meegan stood up and repeatedly slapped him on his chest. "This here"—slap, slap—"is a"—slap—"fucking nigger." She dropped down, laughing.

"May I take your order?" asked the waiter, unaffected by Meegan's outburst.

Augustine was shocked and speechless that her friends had waited for her arrival before ordering their meals.

"Nigga, bring us a bucket of ribs, a box of fries, and a basket of bread. Chop, chop, nig, nig!" ordered Meegan.

The girls giggled at the slave. Augustine covered her mouth, and her stomach ached. No matter how fucked up and snobby Meegan was, she always made her laugh. She needed it. The looming execution was sometimes too much to bear.

"Girl, did you see the one they brought in?" said a brunette. "His dick is *sooo* big."

"Really?" said another.

Speed metal, potent drinks, and stiff cock. Augustine couldn't think of a better way to spend the weekend.

"Yup. My sperm donor was bitching to my mom that he had to"—her voice then mimicked a grumpy old man—"justify to the order why I need more dungeon space."

"Good job keeping a lookout," said Meegan with a high five.

The girl continued. "So, anyway, I went down to the dungeon and took a peek. Abs for days, I'm talking. I wanted to just eat every inch of him."

The waiter returned with the supper. Meegan was the first to dig in. She buried her hands in the fries, knifed four ribs, and chopped a quarter of the bread. "And?"

"And that's it."

"Well, ladies," Meegan said with a mouthful of food. She swallowed a bit and talked with a bubbly cheek. "Our new friend is no mystery. He's none other than Romulus Tanicus. Some Inferno lowlife awaiting trial for plotting the emperor's assassination. That's why I stashed him at Augustine's place."

"What!" said Augustine. "No. My father will kill me."

"He's not for you, stingy. He's for *all of us.*" Meegan sat back and guffawed, trickling food out of her mouth's corners. "Besides, you said yourself that he extended his mission. Which means we have the grounds all to ourselves."

The fact that Meegan had so easily hidden a slave in Augustine's personal quarters meant her title was laughable. In theory, she ruled in her father's absence. But no self-respecting member of the order would obey an eighteen-year-old. And even if she told her father they had refused, he would rub her on the head and say, "It'll be OK. I'll take care of it," which was always a goddamn lie. Should she sanction her best friend for insubordination or just let it be, as always?

"Come on. What do you say we grab a few bottles and go say hello?"

"I'm down."

"Me too."

"Third."

At times Augustine felt Meegan used their friendship to get what she wanted. However, these were the only friends she had. Not many girls had fathers who belonged to the Order of the Serpent. Those who didn't were too afraid or jealous to talk to her. Augustine gave in and said, "Let's do this before any of our parents find out."

▲   ▲   ▲

THE PALACE, PLANET ATHENA—HEPHAESTUS 27, 899 CD

Augustine and her mischievous crew advanced toward the palace's east-wing gate, which was protected by two legionnaires. She noticed that Eon, the planet's moon, had awoken from its slumber to say good night to Helios. The Milky Way's billions of stars radiated in the eternal darkness and off the legionnaires' black armor. As Meegan took the lead, a strong wind combed her locks and carried a rainy scent. Her friend skipped like a schoolgirl, snagging the armed men's attention.

Augustine surveyed the thick clouds traveling in from a starless western sky. She didn't recall the news forecasting any bad weather. She rotated her neck south and saw the same weather pattern.

Maybe they screwed up. Except inaccurate weather forecasts were never an issue. Sentinel held the technology to predict storms hundreds of Athena years from today. More importantly, the storm season occurred closer to Cryon, the Earth-year-long winter month.

Meegan raised her arms, holding a wine bottle, and asked the guards, "You boys need a hand shooting off those big guns?"

Augustine was certain her friend had zero, if any, plans to ever fire a rifle now that she was out of the Centurion Academy. She was the socialite type, who would live off daddy's bank account and die from a botched plastic-surgery procedure.

The soldiers snapped to attention and saluted Augustine, who had stopped at the gate. After she returned the salute, they opened the barrier. The starlight on their armor began to disappear as the winds picked up. The fire blew out in the torches connected to the stone.

Augustine and her friends double-timed it through the gate to her two-story mini mansion next to the main palace. By the time she reached the wooden door, the wind had intensified enough to knock the cinnamon apples off the trees. She saw a guard leave the gate and stare at the cloud formation. He pressed a button on his helmet's side to transmit an indiscernible message.

She unlocked the door and allowed her friends ahead. It took two of them to close it.

"Where did you put him?" asked Augustine. "I swear, if this is what I think it is…"

The teenage floozy swigged from her bottle and smeared her lipstick with her forearm. "Ladies, follow me."

Meegan's ankles twisted walking up the stairs, and the others cackled. "You're so fucking drunk," said a friend.

"No, you are." Meegan belched and vomited on the wall.

"Stupid cunt! You're gonna clean that," said Augustine. She couldn't go through with this.

"Let me go!" ordered Meegan to the ones holding her up. She grabbed ahold of the railing. "Now, now, daddy's little girl. What's the matter? Afraid to get that cherry popped?" She caressed Augustine's chin with a nail and poked out her lips. "Or does the big bad emperor want this pretty little mouth all to himself?"

Augustine struggled not to use her title to sanction Meegan. She shoved her down instead and stomped up the steps. Her friends continued snickering. Meegan surged past Augustine and kicked open the master bedroom's door.

The room was blanketed in a red light. Romulus's wrists and ankles were bound to the bedposts. His mouth was gagged with panties. Whips, chains, and various dominatrix items were neatly stored around the room. Her blood boiled when she saw an authentic Serpent sword on her dresser. Meegan picked the weapon up by its snakeskin grip and licked the blade alongside the gold serpent emblem. She tossed the sword and spat into Romulus's face.

Rain pounded on the roof, and thunder cracked the sky.

Meegan took a candle and dripped hot wax on his forehead. His arms and legs fought to break free. She slithered a finger from his forehead to his underwear, held his hips, and yanked the garment down.

"Who's first?" said Meegan. "I know." She pointed a finger at Augustine.

The emperor's daughter had no other choice. "I order you to stop this at once!"

Two girls held Augustine's arms hostage, and Meegan grabbed a fistful of her hair. They brought the teen to the bed, and Meegan said, "And I order you to suck this cock! Come on, I know how bad you want it. Sniff it!"

Augustine's once-trusted friends forced her face down.

"Mmm. Smells good, don't it? I bet you can't just wait to cram it into that hot little mouth of yours. Can you?"

She couldn't resist any longer. Augustine stuck out the tip of her tongue and flicked Romulus's undershaft.

"Oh, what do we have here? Daddy's virgin princess getting her first taste of some real dick. Lick it and lick good, bitch."

The girls cheered Augustine on. Meegan moved her head in and started sucking the mushroom. The emperor's daughter used the break to lift up her sweaty shirt. She immediately dove in for more. Meegan held the cock upright, and someone eased Augustine's mouth over it. One of her friends moaned. She peeked up to see two naked girls spread out on the king-size bed. One got between the other's legs and buried her face into her sugar wall.

"Why, that's a nice ass you have there," said the brunette.

"Get it, girl," said Meegan. She gave the penis a final lick and fed it to the emperor's daughter.

Augustine felt two soft hands on her hips, and her jeans and panties were lowered. She stepped out the garments and felt a dildo split her vertical lips. Her friend smacked her ass and pumped faster. She worked her immaculate pussy better than she ever could. Romulus's hardened cock dredged into the core of her filled throat. The girl wiggled a finger between her butt cheeks. Drilled in all holes, Augustine was in erotic bliss. Her hot and young noble body had become desecrated.

She felt thunder and heard it rock the home's windows. The two lesbians on the bed began to scissor each other.

Meegan sat on Romulus's face and rocked her hips. "Yeah, yeah. Eat it, boy." She dropped forward, catching herself, and continued straddling his mouth.

Augustine wanted to cross the forbidden line. Her soaked body yearned for more. Her friend pulled the dildo out, and Augustine plopped on Romulus, turning into a cowgirl.

Augustine thrusted her buttocks on Romulus's monster shaft. Meegan sat upright, and the emperor's daughter grabbed two fistfuls of her succulent breasts.

"That's right, you cock whore. Pump that dick. Pump it like you mean it," whispered Augustine's friend into her left ear. She couldn't control herself. The taste of hot dick, the scent of perspiring bodies, and his engorged cock held her hostage. The deflowered princess cried out and velociously moved her noble loins. Her body shivered uncontrollably. As a thick river flowed through her corrupted orifice, everything went black.

WAR OF WARS

THE PALACE, PLANET
ATHENA—HEPHAESTUS 28, 899 CD

A flushed toilet summoned her from an elusive dream. She kept her spinning head on the fluffy pillow. No sunlight greeted her when she opened her eyes. Last night's rain continued to pummel the bedroom window. She flipped on her side to see Meegan sprawled out in a deep snore. Augustine's face squished, getting a whiff of her friend's armpit and lingering alcohol stench.

The brunette came out the bathroom and yawned. She stumbled, and a pillow was thrown from the floor, hitting her in the face.

"What's your deal?" she said. "I'll see you skanks later. My dad this morning just up and decided to send me and my brother to Aquarius for the summer." The girl left the room and hobbled down the staircase.

A squinty-eyed Meegan awoke and sluggishly said, "You really shouldn't leave your diary alone in the library."

Augustine gasped and got out of bed.

"That was some wild fantasy you had there. One down, nine more to go. I am flattered nonetheless."

She had misplaced the diary that held her darkest secrets and desires. Fantasies she was too afraid to indulge in before her execution.

Her friend rolled out of bed as the others slipped from under their sleeping bags. Augustine picked the Serpent Blade up off the floor.

"My dad's. He'll never need it. Probably won't even notice the thing's missing," said Meegan.

She had never expected to hold a Serpent Blade for the first time after raping a male servant. She imagined kneeling before the ancient Roman Order to receive the honor. She felt dirty and full of inescapable guilt. The weapon's legacy was tarnished with her filthy schoolgirl fantasy.

Despite her feelings, Augustine rotated the sword and admired the fanged emblem that ran five inches from the grip's base to midblade on both sides.

"Looks good on you. I'm going to whip up some French toast and eggs." Meegan followed the hungover entourage out the room.

Moments later, Augustine heard a high-pitched scream, which she ignored. Her dainty friends were scared of every furry creature known to man. Anyhow, it was probably the mansion's nine-legged pest saying good morning. She often fed Buster leftovers to keep him from raiding the cupboards at night.

Augustine stepped in front of the walk-in closet's standing mirror. She bent at the waist and cocked her fists, pointing the blade at her naked reflection. "En garde!" The weapon was heavier than she had envisioned, but not enough so to prevent her from slashing an invisible two-headed enemy. She spun around and sliced the creature's heads clean off. Augustine knew the weapon's true power was harnessed only through Serpent Armor.

She exhaled and lowered the sword. She became cognizant of an uncomfortable silence. Her chatty friends were never short of nitwitted gossip. It was a fat chance they'd left. Buster wasn't the only deviant to raid her fridge and cabinets. Rarely did they leave a sleepover on an empty stomach.

Augustine decided she would store the weapon above the bedroom fireplace until breakfast was over. The last thing she needed was for her father to show up and see her with a Serpent Blade. She dressed in blue silk pajamas and descended the white staircase barefoot.

Augustine's forehead dampened, and her lungs sucked in humid air. She began to curse those imbeciles for leaving the front door open. She explored the luxurious kitchen. No bacon sizzling, no coconut coffee brewing, no television blaring. Then the entertainment room. Not even an asinine laugh or loutish joke to be heard.

Where are they?

A rumble moved the mansion, and she seized a leather love seat. Augustine homed in on the screams outside. The soaked women were huddled together just beyond the water fountain. The legionnaires had abandoned their posts.

An immeasurable dark object loomed on the near horizon. Its nose was curved like a bean, and scores of mechanical tentacles extended out its back. The anomaly spurted continuous red charges from its underbelly to the planet's surface. To the far west, she saw three more blasting Utopis. Several people hustled past the unguarded gate; some carried children or whatever they could.

She ran to her friends as they split the huddle. "Meegan, what's going on?"

She shook the girl's bare shoulder. "Meegan?"

"I...I don't know," she whimpered.

"Fuck! What is that thing?" one of the girls asked.

Augustine reckoned the mysterious objects were spacecraft designed by a sentient intelligence. The empire possessed no such technology.

The northern spacecraft were upon the palace. "I want everyone inside, now!" ordered Augustine, hearing Sentinel's fighters close in.

They didn't question the lady's demand. But Meegan stayed behind. "It's happening."

"What? What is happening, Meegan?"

The ship eclipsed the courtyard. The two girls were right beneath the spacecraft's underbelly. A red charge crashed the stone surface, and she blocked a shrapnel trajectory.

The escapees' yowls magnified to stomach-churning levels.

Ice streamed up Augustine's veins. Her chest twisted at the nine-foot-tall, four-legged alien. Its slimy, dark-green skin dripped ooze and was protected by no visible armor. The enemy used the two largest arms of its four to support highly advanced pulsators. The alien's four eyes sat inside an elongated skull that fused with its back. She attested to the weapon's capabilities, observing men, women, and children being roasted alive.

The alien aimed the pulsator's glowing barrel at Augustine, and she charged the enemy, rolling under its incinerating gunfire. She clutched the alien's disgusting forearms, disrupting its aim. The fully automatic weapon went haywire, and Meegan's gut exploded.

Augustine was catapulted into thin air. *Thunk!* Her cranium ricocheted off the water-fountain top, and her lower back ruptured on its porcelain bottom. With half her body inside the artwork, she slipped out of the water. Augustine trundled left and struggled to her hands and knees. Her right temple stung like hell.

The pulsator faced her. A barrage of gunfire dissected the alien's skin. Its large legs collapsed.

"Hurry!" called one of the girls from the window.

There was no doubt her empire—the entire planet—was under attack from an alien invasion.

Augustine ran to Meegan's side. She cradled her head and wiggled an arm under her bloody back.

"Don't bother," she said softly, amid remote fighting. "My father. You have to…" Blood poured from her lip's crevices. "Save us. Save the empire."

Meegan closed her eyes.

"Augustine, they're coming!"

Six aliens converged on the small mansion. Incendiary bullets tore at the house's stone. Her friends retaliated, and she used the onslaught as cover.

The enemy let out sickening gurgles from lead penetrating their torsos. Before Augustine reached the steps, she looked back to see her pursuers. An alien shot an energized projectile from a pack attached to its back.

Boom!

The mansion's top floor fragmented. A second projectile brought it down. Her friends murdered in cold blood by vile savages. Augustine covered her face and rushed forth into the fumes. She shed no tears for the girls, who were crushed under stone. The aliens understood only death and heartlessness. She needed to match them with the same callous punishment that had killed her friends. Today, she would die on her feet—like the empress, who had refused to die for becoming pregnant with her brother.

Augustine took concealment in the war's fog. The aliens' slow movement was evidence they came from a gravity-dense home world. She used their weakness to search the wreckage for weaponry.

Augustine pried a Spectra-800 semiautomatic rifle from a dismembered hand and wreaked vengeance into the accumulating smoke. They struck back, and she sought cover behind stone. A lull in the fighting ensued. She auscultated the aliens' position by their squishy footsteps and deep snore-like inhalations through a single nostril. She remained crouched and saw a shiny object that was illuminated by crackling fire.

The blade.

An alien's gargantuan leg blocked the fire's light. A slew of rounds traveled up its spine, revealing her position. She scurried to the dead alien and swooped up the sword. She ran toward the familiar amber light and high-pitched sound. Augustine channeled hate and patriotism into a single trigger pull aimed at its stomach. Gunk splashed her face as the Serpent Blade lacerated its organs.

She pushed through the smoke, slicing and dicing alien limbs. Covered in unimaginable shit, Augustine fought for her freedom. She fought for her dead friends. She fought for the empire.

She disemboweled the final invader with a 360-degree chop across his abdomen. The demon's upper half spat grayish guts and bile.

Legionnaire transmissions and chatter came her way. She assumed a fighting stance with the Spectra-800 in one hand and the blade in the other. Multiple legionnaires appeared through the smoke, rain, and fire.

"My lady, the empire's under attack. The emperor has ordered us to move you to safety under the palace. Please come with us."

The legionnaire's spiked black shoulder pads informed her that he was their leader. "Your name?"

"Master Legionnaire Codex," he said.

Her secret passage was impassable. They'd have to fight their way around the palace.

"Who are they? And how many of the emperor's people have died?"

Bombs and machine-gun fire were all around her.

Codex replied, "We don't know, ma'am. Tens, maybe hundreds of thousands."

He outfitted her chest in a bronze muscle cuirass with shoulder pads. "I'll carry my own," she snapped at him when he tried to lighten her load.

She aimed the Spectra-800 at a ninety-degree angle; sheathed the Serpent Blade on her back, between her shoulder blades; and ran with the men past the destroyed gate.

Severed limbs and burnt intestines were strewn in every direction. Vehicles were missing entire backsides, and their occupants were smoldering crisps. Shops and various structures were aflame.

A lone boy, in ripped clothing, hightailed it in her direction. She watched him look back for any pursuers.

"My lady," he called, with his arms out for her.

"Halt! Face down!" commanded Codex.

The boy immediately complied.

"I dare you!" She shoved his barrel away and ran to the child's aid. "On your feet, boy." She turned to her escorts and said, "The emperor's people are not the enemy. Especially these children." She pointed to the spaceship hovering in distant dark clouds. "Those are who we must fight. Hand him a weapon."

A legionnaire relinquished a side arm to the boy.

"My boy, where are your mother and father?"

He returned his eyes the way he'd come.

She directed Codex to call for a craft. "We need to get him to safety."

"Trinity, this is Phoenix Squad leader."

"Phoenix Squad, you recover and deliver the package?" transmitted the outpost's battlefield controller (BFC).

"Affirmative. Ready for evac," he said, lying, and then he spoke to Augustine. "Our Air Defense Fighter bases have their hands full. Nobility has become priority number one. Wounded military and civilians second."

"Where are we taking them?" asked Augustine.

"The emperor issued a planetwide evacuation of all survivors to outposts. The closest one to our position is Trinity." Not only was Outpost Trinity incapable of mounting a sustainable defense, but also its weapon systems were toys in comparison to what she'd seen so far.

"Then that's where we're headed."

"My lady. Your father—"

"To hell with your orders, Legionnaire! I'm not going to sit on my ass while the empire's being overrun by the gods know what." She was giving them no other choice. She and the legionnaires proceeded down the wet and body-littered street. She watched the sky and noticed the spacecraft had become stationary.

The BFC came back. "Incoming coordinates." Codex rotated his gauntlet and checked his digital SpecNav.

"We got a quarter mile, maybe more. If we're not there by touchdown, we'll be humping it the rest of the way."

Augustine's weapon was at a steady Weaver-ready. All her training had never accounted for a full-fledged military invasion by an alien force. This war was not going to end well.

The rain intensified, and her bare feet stepped in blood, guts, brains, and sausage-linked intestines. Fried bodies and vehicles created smoke that lessened visibility. Inhuman shadows were upon them.

"Enemy," warned a legionnaire. "Twelve o'clock."

They sought protection at the sides of combusted rovers.

She observed their movements from behind cover. "Wait," she said, watching the invaders pause in the middle of the road. One after the other, they inhaled deeply. She realized this was not a respiratory function but rather an evolved form of communication. One spoke more often, and his inhalations were noticeably more ferocious.

"Leave the one in the center to me," said Augustine.

Codex threw up hand signals, and his soldiers stayed low while spreading out.

"Let 'em have it!" she cried.

Spectras and pulsators went to war.

Augustine fired at the ones trying to protect the infantry's unarmed leader, who wore a metallic harness shaped like an octagon in the center. The extraterrestrials surrounded the alien in an effort to push back. "Take 'em down, now!"

Incendiary bullets pinged off the vehicles.

As Augustine discharged her weapon from behind cover, an alien began to power the energy launcher.

"Target that grenadier!" she yelled while blitzing their defenses.

The launcher glowed a bright amber. The legionnaires reloaded and fired at the aliens to the front and flanks.

"Cover me!" Augustine took flight over the rover's hood and mowed the creatures. The legionnaires laid down suppressive fire. Her weapon automatically released the empty mag. The grenadier's left front and hind legs gave out. She retrieved the Serpent Blade and torpedoed it at the alien's burly chest. He fell on his backside.

"Advance!"

Her men were on the assault. The invaders' numbers dwindled drastically. They'd counted on the grenadier to finish the attack.

The leader's last line of defense was dead.

Augustine stepped on the dead grenadier's stomach and extracted the oozing blade from its body.

She fast-paced it to the unguarded leader.

"My lady!"

She heeded no caution and slashed away, rendering it paraplegic. The alien cried through its tiny mouth and slunk over, bleeding. This one was bigger than those he'd commanded.

"My lady." She heard boots run up behind her.

The alien's four beady eyes stared back. The Serpent Blade's end pricked its neck.

"I am Augustine Claudius, daughter of the emperor. Why have you come here? I demand that you answer me!"

The creature inhaled loudly. Digital alien hieroglyphics continuously changed shape in the octagon.

"Ma'am, there's no time," said Codex.

Whoever they were and wherever they'd come from, they did not come in peace. She punctured the alien's neck and twisted the blade until its eyes became still.

Augustine listened to the air being sucked out near her. She turned and saw the boy collapse. The legionnaires blew away the alien, who'd fired the fatal shot on its side. The child was dead, and there was nothing else she could do for him.

She saw a Devil's Wing's four front lights a short distance away.

"That's our ride, men. Hustle up!" yelled Codex.

Augustine and the legionnaires double-timed up the flooded streets to the evac point. The sleek and black Devil's Wing rotated and started its descent. As she stood and watched it land, she felt her throbbing soles' open lacerations soak up grit and water.

The aircraft's rear hatch rose. Codex escorted Augustine in first and entered after the last man.

▲   ▲   ▲

Outpost Trinity, Planet Athena— Hephaestus 28, 899 CD

The Devil's Wing landed forty minutes later at the outpost. When the ramp lowered, a squad of legionnaires and medical personnel were waiting on the tarmac. Two white coats stood by with a stretcher. Augustine guessed that the pilot had notified the BFC that she was on board, without her knowledge.

The entire way here, she had kept her feet on the cold floor, careful not to move them. Hardly a word had been spoken between any of them. She imagined that deep down inside, the men were just as scared as regular civilians. Somewhere in this caliginous hour of war were their families, awaiting their arrival. Yet the men pushed on.

Codex's troops departed the craft, leaving him with her. The medical staff rolled the stretcher onto the Devil's Wing. They relieved Augustine of her gear and released it to Codex. Two staff members lifted her by the armpits and legs and rested her body on the stretcher. Codex didn't say a word as they wheeled her into the downpour. She saw skeleton crews loading onto Devil's Wings, track-wheeled combat-support vehicles (CSVs) forwarding off to battle, and legionnaires manning a turret atop a nearby tower.

Shortly thereafter, in the infirmary, an older male doctor applied the last bandage on her right foot. The medical team had moved her to a private area, away from the grunts who were being stitched back together. "All done. Stay off them till morning to let the wounds heal properly." She nodded. "Take two of these. You'll see they work like magic." He smiled and handed her a pill bottle.

"You're mighty chirpy for someone who's at war," she said.

The doctor fixed his glasses and said, "My apologies, my lady."

"And that goes for the rest of you." She directed her stare at a black-haired nurse seated at a table texting on her transmitter. "What is your mission?" asked Augustine.

"I maintain staff records."

"Wrong. You"—she looked at two more loitering bodies—"you, and you. I want you armed and on the battlefield. Now!"

They moved out the door as ordered.

A fourth nurse prepped a wheelchair and positioned it next to the bed. "What is this, a fucking taxi service? Saddle up!" she commanded the woman, causing her to run out of the room.

"My lady, I mean no disrespect, but my staff is already undermanned. They need all the help I can muster," said the doctor.

"Grab a weapon and provide it for them."

He sighed. "Very well."

"Do you have any business here?" asked a second doctor, opening the glass door to address a legionnaire and let the first doctor pass. "This area is off-limits. If you need meds, put your name on the list at the front desk. Critically wounded take priority."

As the doctor started to close the door, Augustine recognized the familiar spiked shoulder pads. "Wait," she said. "He's with me."

The physician adjusted his spectacles and went back to filling out paper work.

This man was responsible for saving her life. The least she could do was acknowledge his presence.

"Pardon the intrusion, my lady. I...I just wanted to see how you were doing."

"You have my gratitude, Legionnaire. We can drop the formalities. You've earned that right."

She listened to him breathe under the black helmet. "Can I see the face to which I am in debt?"

Codex pressed two buttons on opposite sides of his neck, releasing the air, and then he removed the helmet. She guessed his age at around thirty. He wore a shadow faded high and tight that matched his hazelnut eyes.

"Your tent is ready," reported an unarmored legionnaire. His black military uniform's sleeves were rolled up, and a medical badge dangled from his neck. Whatever threat they were facing, it was in everyone's best interest to protect themselves. The aliens saw all human life as an enemy.

Codex guided Augustine through the open door held by the medical staffer. He turned the wheelchair right and headed deeper into the open hangar. The rain's heavy stench clogged her nostrils, and she listened to it pound the tarmac outside. A spare body kept the door at the back of the hangar that led to tent city. Codex quickened his step toward a lone tent on its own row. Two legionnaires who stood fast at the entrance pulled the handle and allowed them through.

An emperor-size bed, 3-D television, refrigerator, private immobile transmitter (IT), couch, and clothes chest. She was well aware of her two-piece family's overprivileged lifestyle.

"I hope this is to your comfort level. Me and my men are scheduled for mission debrief," said Codex.

She rolled forward a few feet and rotated the chair. "You're missing a gun. I'm assuming he was killed." Centurions were in charge of leading legionnaire outfits in times of war.

"Kid froze up when my squad made first contact. Never fired a single round."

"I'm sorry to hear that."

"Don't be. I would have shot him myself, if they hadn't." The young centurions were unpopular among the hardened legionnaire ranks, due to their lack of experience.

"Good day, ma'am. Rest well."

The empire was at war, and here she was, sidelined by a chipped toenail. She wheeled herself over to the holographic television window and pressed the 3-D power button. A blond newscaster, embedded in an infantry unit, reported the action live from downtown Utopis. A muscle cuirass covered her vital organs as she tagged behind riflemen. "The entire city has been overrun by an unknown extraterrestrial civilization. Much of their efforts are concentrated here in the downtown region." Legionnaires fired their rifles and were seen weaving between demolished buildings and taking cover anywhere they could find. "If you are listening to this broadcast, we urge you to get to your nearest outpost."

A crouched legionnaire turned around and commanded, "Get down!"

An amber glow appeared in the downpour. She covered her face, and the camera dropped.

Static.

Operation: Firestorm

Outpost Trinity, Planet Athena— Hephaestus 29, 899 CD

"All combat-support squads report to the briefing tent by zero six thirty hours. All combat-support squads report to the briefing tent by zero six thirty hours," the camp loudspeaker announced.

Codex scooted up in bed and massaged his temples.

The tent flapped open, and an unseasonably hot and suffocating breeze circulated. "Master Legionnaire—"

"Yeah, I heard. Thanks." He consulted his watch: 0515 hours. Today was going to be a good day. They had left him enough time for breakfast and a hot shower.

The flap closed, and it was dark again.

"Rise and shine, boys." His sleepy outfit grumbled, and bunks squeaked. "Shit, shower, shave, grab a banana, and gear up." Codex undressed, put on his shower shoes, and proceeded outside.

His chest became heavy, and his legs stiffened. The atmosphere wanted to crush his lungs. He studied the overcast hanging above him and wiped his brow.

He entered the shower tent to rooting and chanting. Sergeant Bryana Vitoria good gamed him on the ass as he found an unused shower head. The bald and shredded heavy gunner began to sing a popular R and B song. "I would die just to feel you next to me." The whole gang joined in. "Can't you see…"

"All right, all right," said Codex, smiling. He lathered the back of his neck and stomach. "You made your point."

"You ain't going soft on us, are you?" asked Bryana. "I mean, how can she just bark orders at us like that?"

"Keep in mind, she is nobility. So behave, at least while she's here."

"She's a centurion by default. No way they'd fail her," said another squad member.

He shook his head. "Default or not, the woman knows how to fight."

Bryana shut off her shower head. "You can't be serious. Bitch can barely swing a sword. And it wasn't even hers. It belonged to a Serpent."

"Bet she can swing a dick," joked a soldier next to Bryana. "In her mouth!"

Bryana grabbed the man's cock and jiggled it.

Everyone laughed.

She let him loose. "She has to go. No ifs, ands, or butts. We don't get paid to babysit."

Codex needed to keep his squad in good spirits. The war and their lives counted on it. "We'll go out, and by the time we get back, I'm positive she'll be gone."

"Did you see her tent? Fucking Christ. I wish I was born with a pink twat and shat coin," said another.

Normally, Codex didn't care if his crew spouted shit about the centurions. In his fifteen-Earth-year career, they had come and gone. Augustine was different. She *did* hold her own. Better than anyone he'd fought alongside.

"You guys dry off and hit the grab 'n' go," said Codex, keeping a straight face. They followed the order, with Bryana leaving last and meeting him eye to eye.

He didn't struggle admitting to himself that he needed Augustine on his team. But how would he convince the outpost commander to allow the emperor's only daughter to accompany him in battle? The decision wouldn't be the commander's to begin with. That would be left to her father, who hadn't addressed the planet as of yet—or Kronos, for that matter. Bits and pieces came from administrators hiding in the safety of Aquarius's deep ocean. His only hope was to ask her himself.

Forty minutes later, Codex watched his men file into the large and packed briefing tent and take their places next to riflemen, centurions, and other master legionnaires. "Move it, people. Remember, you're on time, you're late."

The team's only sergeant sat down in the last row. She folded her arms, tapped her feet, and looked the other way.

High-ranking legionnaires entered the tent, bearing the ranks of sergeant major legionnaire and major legionnaire.

"Squad," said Codex, "atten-hooah!"

The tent shot to attention. Command Sergeant Major Legionnaire (CSMl) Ariel Lucas broke the threshold.

"At ease," the tan-skinned female said, walking up the aisle.

This was a surprise. The legionnaires' highest-ranking leader rarely showed her face in any capacity around the grunts. That was, unless she was smiling for the news media to boost her undeserved ego. Codex didn't see any reporters. So whatever it was, it must've been important.

Ariel took a position at the podium, which was in front of a big, blank holographic screen. The lights dimmed. "I'm sure you all felt what I did when you woke up this morning. The same for those of you coming off shift."

A second later, black-and-white satellite imagery showed an obelisk-like object under a heavy cloud formation. "Intelligence believes this object is being used to terraform our atmosphere. Athena's gravity density has increased drastically since the object's arrival, in Drakon's Rock, less than five hours ago. Thirty percent in some areas and fifty percent in others. Our artillery and fighter squadrons have thrown everything at their disposal at it, to no effect."

Codex knew where this was going, and it wasn't good. To his knowledge, there was one weapon powerful enough to blow the hell out of the alien terraformer.

Lucas continued her briefing. "We need support teams to ensure our infantrymen can get close enough to deploy the SGM-100T. You'll have whatever air support can be provided."

Shit, she's out of her damn mind.

The room was dead.

"Expect heavy resistance. You'll be linking up with Ground Assault Forces from the First GAF Legion and some squads from your own." She seemed to address Codex, who was at the back of the tent, when she looked his way. "The success of this mission rests on all of us. Especially our support squads."

GAFs were nothing more than trigger-happy bullet catchers. He used to be one until he lost his marbles and purchased a five-thousand-coin engagement ring. One year later, he was changing diapers and dreading the hour-long drive to his monotonous logistics position at the Fifth Combat Support Legion. Ironically, the invasion was giving him what he'd missed the most—fresh air.

"Operation: Firestorm goes into effect at eleven hundred hours. This is it. Keep your heads down and shoot straight."

Augustine squatted and wrapped her gloved hands around the barbell. With sweat seeping from every pore, she rose and arched her back. Her traps cried for mercy, fighting against six forty-five-pound plates.

Clank. She repeated the movement.

Last rep. "Rrgh!" The weights clashed against the mat.

She interlaced her fingers behind her soaked long hair and turned her attention to the ceiling. The pain pills were a godsend. She didn't have any intention of staying put. She was well recovered and ready to hit the streets.

The main door's knob twisted. The outpost's commander refused to allow Augustine to walk the post unguarded. Two men stood outside the gym tent to prevent anyone else from entering. She had a hunch as to who might have convinced them otherwise.

She retrieved two eighty-pound dumbbells off the rack and pushed out a set of standing bicep curls, watching the door through the mirror. She noticed her strength and recover time had vastly improved over the past month. Her two-mile run was a little under thirteen minutes, and her squat max had rocketed to 340. She observed her six-pack under the wet white sports bra and her semithick calves. Every workout was cakewalk.

"I see you're feeling better," he said.

"Can't you tell? Maybe later today I'll give your tomboy some lessons on swinging dick."

There was a pause before Codex said, "Sergeant Vitoria… well…the invasion took a lot from her."

"Must be heartbreaking to know you're the only one who lost something." Augustine reracked the weights and moved to a flat bench, never looking at Codex. She slid under the barbell and heaved 405 above her chest. She pushed out five reps and reracked. Sitting up, she said, "Hope you saved everyone else some hot water, because I could really use a shower."

"Augustine, I'm not going to apologize for what was said. They're grown men and women, and that's their responsibility."

"Then what *did* you come here for?" She went back under for more.

"We're going back out on a mission. At eleven hundred hours, Sentinel is carrying out an attack forty miles east of the outpost."

"Drakon's Rock. Word gets around. I've mapped it." The mountainous region was named for the morbid two-winged beasts that scoured the lands for human flesh. In her studies of ancient Earth, she had learned of tales that fictionalized the creature. Who would have known that the nightmare-inducing phenoms were real, a mere 12.4 light-years away?

"You cannot go out there alone. It's far too risky. We're already getting our asses handed to us."

She sat up and then walked to her open gym bag to snag her shaker bottle. She uncapped it and sucked down chocolate protein she had found in her tent's cabinet.

"The First GAF Legion are deploying an SGM-100T near an alien terraformer."

This time she looked at Codex.

"I know. It's suicide, but we're gonna need a good leader."

The blast circumference and force of a space-guided missile was large enough to level the Sentinel battle station twice over.

"From what I can tell, this is high above Lucas's paygrade," Codex said.

"So just come out and say it."

Codex shied away and then refocused. "I'm not placing the blame on your father."

"Who, then?"

Codex didn't answer.

"Exactly." Augustine picked up her gym bag, walked to the exit, and shoved open the door.

The morning's humidity started to triple the amount of water soaking her workout clothes, which bore the Sentinel Centurion Academy's black galea logo on the upper right breast and lower right thigh. "Stand down," she ordered the legionnaires, who tried following her.

"Wait," Codex said, grabbing her sweaty arm to turn her around. He scanned the grounds, as though he expected to be arrested for assault.

"My lady, is everything all right?" asked a passing centurion who held his galea. The other hand hovered near his drop holster.

She shook her head slightly, peering into Codex's eyes. "Yes, thank you, good sir."

Codex came closer and, in a low tone, said, "We need a strong sword. Don't make me have to explain combat basics to whatever entitled kid they throw my way. The outpost commander is not sending any squads on mission without a centurion."

"Entitled, am I?" She started to walk away, but he stopped her once more.

"That's…that's not what I…" He put his hands on his hips. "Look, if you change your mind, we move out at eleven hundred hours." He nodded in the direction of a one-level hardened structure some meters to his left. He turned and headed off.

She knew Codex wasn't going to be reduced to begging. As kindhearted as he was to her, he was, nonetheless, a warrior by trade.

She skipped the shower and returned to her tent.

She humphed and raised an eyebrow at a sleeveless black muscle cuirass and the matching cape, gauntlets, galea, shield, and boots on her bed. The Serpent Blade next to it had been spit shined.

She wasn't at all surprised the grunts regarded her as nothing more than a thrill-seeking spoiled teenager. They'd spent their careers in the trenches, training for this day. Perhaps she would be the one shot by friendly fire if she agreed to Codex's request. *Grow the fuck up*, she told herself, noticing she was starting to sound like Meegan on her best days. She tied her hair into a bun and suited up.

"Incoming urgent transmission from Emperor Claudius. Accept or deny," sounded the transmitter affixed to her in-tent desk.

She laced up her last boot and replied, "Accept."

"Analyzing vocal pattern. Good morning, my lady. Connecting call."

Emperor Claudius's face maximized in a hologram.

She pretended to care. "Are you safe?"

"I'm well. I became worried, learning you never reported to the palace. But less about me. How have you held up?"

"The grounds were overrun with enemy. They escorted me to Trinity, and here I am." She left out the part about her slicing extraterrestrials in half with a Serpent Blade.

"I'm afraid you'll have to stay put a little while longer. All air-evac operations have been suspended." Which meant he was still on the planet. "As soon as we have control of the airspace, I'll arrange for your extradition to Aquarius."

"That won't be necessary, Father. I've been assigned to Phoenix Squad as the centurion in charge. I need to know why we've been invaded."

The emperor sighed, and his eyebrows slanted. She felt a cold chill when he said, "You will do as I say!"

"People are dying. Your *men* are dying."

"Do not put it past me to chain you, at your age."

The emperor's threatening tone was the likeness of when he used to "discipline" her in his private chambers. She recalled the malodor of hard whiskey and sting of his spiked whip. It was this child abuser who was responsible for her mother's death. She remembered the lies he once told her five-year-old self that the empress had passed away from of a mysterious illness. It was only later that she found out through Kronos the truth. The eternals forbade the last empress in the bloodline from bearing a male child. To do so would upset the bloodline and cause the rightful child, and his offspring, to wage endless war against the throne. Her mother, who was captured in hiding, fought to her dying breath, sending the emperor's men to their deaths. Kronos told her how her father's sword pierced the empress's womb. Her father was unaware that she knew it was he who had sealed her defiant mother's fate.

"I love you," he said.

She shoved all the years of pain and torment into two words. "Fuck you." Augustine shut off the hologram.

Her chest heaved, and her fists balled up as she reminisced about her childhood. She only respected the emperor in public and had never loved her father the way he wanted her to.

Not the way she had adored her mother. Augustine could never forgive him for what he'd done. His belittling words and heavy-handed admonishments were dealt to crush her soul.

She recalled the night the motherfucker shaved her head and locked her in a chest for two days without food for kissing her first crush—a handsome slave boy her age. The emperor caught her making out with the boy in the garden and ordered him to be hog roasted on a spit for his family's breakfast. The husband and wife refused and were taken to Drakon's Rock to be crucified. Their hanging bodies were left for the two-winged beasts. She remembered waiting in darkness and listening to how their deaths were her fault. The emperor referred to her by the vilest of names. Men came and went pissing, vomiting, shitting, and ejaculating into the air hole of the chest to defile her.

I will not be broken. Augustine grabbed the sword and bashed the tent door open with her fist.

She walked with haste toward the armory.

She started to remember the empress, before her death, teaching her that no matter what, she needed to be strong. That one day she would discover the dark beauty of her inner self and to be ruthlessness against those who threatened it. To always seek unchallenged power but never neglect to use her heart at the right time. This war needed a true leader. Not a pedophilic fuck wearing a crown made of shit.

Augustine watched soldiers clap ammo clips into magazine wells and strap on fresh gear. The troops were more concerned with their armament than Augustine's presence—except for the handful of centurions who gave a respectful nod. This placed her at ease.

She eyed Codex conversing with Bryana, both fully geared—with the exception of their helmets—at the armory's far end. As Augustine stepped closer, the master legion-naire's troops' heads moved in another direction. One of them grinned, placed his hand behind his high-and-tight, and walked away.

Bryana, finally noticing Augustine, folded her arms and repositioned on Codex's right. He moved to a locker and fisted it one time, prying it open. "Couldn't find any laying around, but your predecessor just went on extended leave. Don't expect he'll be back anytime soon."

Augustine removed the Spectra-700 and drop holster from the locker and connected it to her right thigh. The weapon retracted. The Spectra-700's retractable feature allowed a cen-turion to use a sword and shield in battle without having to hold the rifle.

Codex didn't appear ecstatic she'd opted to join his squad, and she didn't expect him to be. He kept a straight face while looking over his weapon. He wasn't going to hold a gun to her head or give her a good pounding between the sheets to per-suade her. Though she wouldn't mind the latter. She admired his rough outer shell, and his broken compassion stole her heart. She saw the light-skinned woman in the picture hang-ing inside his locker watching her. He took the picture and stuffed it under his cuirass.

"Room, atten-hooah!" called out an unfamiliar centurion. Ariel and First Centurion Vlad Hexgrm, the outpost commander, approached Augustine and Codex.

"What is the meaning of this shit you're pulling, Legionnaire?" asked Ariel. "I don't recall giving you authorization to speak with nobility."

Codex looked at Augustine and then lowered his brow.

"Pardon this legionnaire's boldness, my lady, I ask of you."

Codex straightened up, and Lucas's head lifted slightly.

Augustine nodded at Codex and said, "Master Legionnaire."

"Load up!" he commanded.

The troops filed out a double back door to the running CSVs. Augustine eyed Ariel and Vlad one last time before following the team out. No sooner had she stepped out of the armory than the two were on her ass.

"My lady, please reconsider this," said Ariel. "We are under strict orders to ensure your well-being until it is safe for you to depart."

Augustine saw the squad move up the vehicles' ramps. "Then grab a gun and join the fucking party." She had no time for any more bullshit. Her friends were dead, the empire was all but destroyed, and there were Athenians dying out there. She reached the first CSV and stopped at the ramp. A legionnaire hustled by her and into the vehicle.

"We are unclear as to their true capabilities and cannot promise their defeat, or your survival, once the SMGs launch from Eon," said Ariel.

"Well, I can. I'm marching into the heart of Drakon's Rock to take back what belongs to the empire." Augustine started up the ramp and halted. She looked over her shoulder and said, "I suggest you do the same."

She stepped on board, and the ramp raised shut.

▲   ▲   ▲

Drakon's Rock, Planet Athena— Hephaestus 29, 899 CD

For the past thirty minutes, Phoenix Squad had been traveling over Drakon's Rock's unforgiving terrain. She knew that by now, they were deep into the mountains.

She used the holographic map that was positioned in the center of the troop bay to observe the uneven road and cliffs that bordered it. This avenue of approach would be used by the GAF infantrymen, who were several klicks behind her unit.

And there it was, miles ahead. An azure light projected into a dismal and gray sky, blackening the space around it. The CSV's driver guided the armored vehicle to the right and sped toward the cliff's slanted and rock-encumbered base. He applied the brake, sending the vehicle into a controlled slide. Harnesses unlocked. The hatch lowered and thudded on solid and loose rock.

She unlatched her harness and followed two legionnaires out and down the ramp. She detached the Serpent Blade from the cuirass's rear sheath.

Other squad members deployed from separate CSVs.

Sweat secreted out her neck and brow. Her heart squeezed in her chest. "All fire teams, wedge heavy left. Scan closely and kill anything that has more than two legs," she transmitted, using the gauntlet's SpecNav. The fourteen-man team executed the formation. Codex joined Bravo fire team, and Augustine connected with Alpha on point. She wanted to be among the first to blast these assholes back to where they came from. She pointed two fingers ahead, and they marched out.

"So what do you think they're after?" transmitted Codex into her galea's internal earpiece.

"Your guess is better than mine, but what I do know is that I'll be damned if I'm going to give it to 'em." Augustine and her armored comrades continued up the cliff's side.

The skies were noticeably clear of shrilling drakons. The Elders' Decree had recently outlawed unlicensed hunting of the endangered species, but that didn't discourage daring peasants, as her father referred to them, from climbing the deadly rocks to line their pockets. Drakon scales made for the finest clothes sold on the Nexus, a digital network linking the planet. Their meat was the tenderest she'd ever tasted as a little girl, and their heads were multimillion-coin badges of honor. The drakons' absence wasn't a result of illegal hunting. Her gut told her that they'd suffered a fate much worse. The atmosphere was too heavy for them.

Krrrrr! Krr! Krr! Krr! A roaring fighter's engine grew closer. The slanted and black-winged phantom soared over the unit and was followed by five more. "That's our boys!" radioed Codex. "Alpha, let's step it up."

Doon, doon, doon, doon! The fighters' arsenal prepped the way for the infantry.

Augustine's heart pounded as she ran up the cliff's final stretch to flattened land. She felt her mouth salivate at the thought of seeing bits and pieces of aliens scattered...

"Enemy contact, twelve o'clock!" she transmitted. The heroine blocked sizzling bullets with her shield and charged for the closest alien, who was guarding the cliff's top.

"Rrrgh!" She disemboweled him and swung the blade right to slice off an alien's arms.

Amber rounds whizzed past her as her team returned fire. A manned antiaircraft weapon discharged flashes at the circling fighters.

"Phoenix Squad, Phantom-121. Danger close, danger close," transmitted a pilot.

Pfp! Pfp! Pfp! Pfp! Pfp! Pfp!

Augustine ordered, "Keep firing!" while shrapnel pelted her shield and armor. The aliens' AA gun detonated.

Three grenadiers stepped forward with charged packs. She ran and slid behind a pile of large rocks. Portions chipped away from a grenade's impact. She felt as though her veins were on fire. She performed a vertical jump, caught the top of the rock with her sword hand, catapulted, and landed between six aliens. Cut, slash, slice, dice, stab! She was bloodthirsty. Born for war! She carved the invaders into undiscernible parts. An extraterrestrial's entire frame was chopped in half from the head down.

"Suck my fucking dick, you batch of fucking bitches!" transmitted Bryana from Charlie fire team. Augustine detected the heavy machine gunner's continuous and rapid response to the invasion.

"Trinity to all support teams. GAF are proceeding up to target."

"Trinity, Phantom-121 copies. Phoenix Squad, danger close, danger close."

Augustine listened and watched two fighters split formation in midair. One aimed for the left cliff's topside. The other shredded the sparse gathering of aliens who sat in her sights.

"The empire stands with you. Fight for your family. Fight for Rome!" Augustine and her team slaughtered the remainder and charged toward the cliff's far left edge. She took a knee, reattached the sword, and used the Spectra-700 to zoom in on the alien force blocking the GAF's advance.

Tff! Tff! Tff! Tff! Tff! Tff! Tff! Tff!

"Reloading," hollered Bryana.

Clink, chank. Tff! Tff! Tff! Tff! Tff! Tff! Tff! Tff!

Bryana's rounds shifted and annihilated scores of aliens.

Augustine found head targets, killing them instantly. This was total war. The GAF trucked onward, and, as expected, many succumbed to death, and those who didn't wished they had. Some cowered behind rocks in the fetal position, praying for this to end. Any number of them could have been carrying transmitters. The approach was a violent, fatal funnel. For every alien she sent under, ten of her people would never make it. The world itself slowed down with each squeeze of her trigger as tunnel vision settled in. A creeping buzz neared her ear, and the legionnaire squatting next to her spilled backward, sucking her from a soundless void.

She called, "Medic!" She turned and dropped to a knee alongside the young woman, whose neck spouted blood. Augustine released the air from the injured's helmet and removed it. Gear jangled in her direction.

"You'll be fine," said the medic. He covered the wound with a beige cloth to stop the bleeding. She coughed up blood, and he stabbed the other side of her neck with a syringe laced with morphine. A second jab released a concoction that closed her eyes. He waited some seconds and removed the cloth. The woman's skin began to stitch itself. The fix was temporary until she could undergo a full-blown operation.

"I'm out," said a legionnaire, and he was immediately tossed two spare magazines.

"Holy shit," said the medic, watching the western sky. "Reinforcements."

"Get her to safety," said Augustine.

Codex hustled her way. "We gotta get off this cliff!" he yelled over gunfire.

"We stand, and we fight! That's an order. Move!" commanded Augustine.

The slow-moving alien ship dispersed the thick cloud formation thousands of meters to her left. A hornlike sound shock waved from the ship's direction.

"Trinity to all phantoms. Incoming alien craft. Prepare to engage."

The phantoms' twin starburners sonic boomed to counter the threat.

"Phoenix lead to all fire teams. Continue to engage," transmitted Codex.

"Scratch that order, Phoenix lead. You are to disengage immediately. Trinity to all responding forces, fall back. I repeat, fall back."

"Fuck your orders," said Augustine.

"Roger that, ma'am," replied the master legionnaire.

Continued engagement was a certifiable death wish. She witnessed the greenish-black, bean-shaped ship's tentacles fire a barrage of amber missiles. Phantom fighters exploded in midair. Today, the empire would live.

"Trinity, this is Centurion Claudius. Give the order to all units to continue engagement. Now!"

"What are you doing?" Codex sternly asked. "We need to fall back! You're going to get these men killed."

"Do not ever question my decisions, Legionnaire. And how dare you dishonor the empire in my presence! Deploy these soldiers down this cliff. We will end this or die trying."

Codex and Augustine ran to the edge and jumped. She sporadically used her gauntlet's depressurizing system to control her descent.

Her boots touched loose gravel, and she slid on her ass the rest of the way. Immediately, she wasted five invaders who closed in.

The two discharged their weapons and joined the assaulting GAF. She took a knee next to a dead legionnaire and patted down his gear. "What am I looking for?"

"A pentagram-shaped—"

"Got it," she said, locating the connected device on the legionnaire's right hip. She detached the SGM-100T and connected it to an open connector on her hip.

She heard a click, discarded the rifle, and unsheathed the Serpent Blade. A heavy gun sounded behind her.

"Fuck yes, ma'am! We fight for Rome!" transmitted Bryana. She ran up to an alien, shoved the weapon into his stomach, and fired.

"Cover her!" directed Codex.

Augustine's target was the metallic volcano-shaped structure three hundred yards ahead. She sprinted as fast as she could while simultaneously dismembering and splitting aliens in half.

"I'm right…behind you," said Codex.

Trinity continued its transmission to engaging units. The alien ship created a second sound wave that radiated up her back.

"Phantom-121 still in flight. Danger close, danger close." Multiple invaders convulsed and dropped in flames.

Augustine hit an invisible barrier and fell sideways. She stood up and sheathed the sword.

Bryana's rounds ricocheted, dispersing the force field's red currents in various directions. The aliens in the field watched and stepped back. Other soldiers arrived to investigate the anomaly.

"It was a trap. We would have never made it," said Codex.

Bryana shouted, "Fuck you!" at the aliens and punched the force field.

"Let's see how they like this," said Augustine. She tossed the SGM-100T on the dirt and looked back at the encroaching ship. "Trinity, contact Eon. Weapon deployed."

"We got five minutes before this place is a goddamn sandbox," said Bryana.

"Hey, boss," said a legionnaire. "Cave. Twenty-six hundred meters."

"Good looking, soldier. Let's get at it." GAF and additional support units left to escape the incoming blast.

Augustine and the remaining squad members hustled to a cave only a few meters away. As she got closer, the open entrance appeared to be geometrically constructed. The top resembled that of a large triangular door. They hurried in, with Augustine covering for the last man.

"We're not going too far. Damn thing's been sealed off," said a legionnaire as he hit a wall of solid dirt twenty feet in.

The horn sounded again, and Augustine stepped outside in the spaceship's shadow.

"Fifteen seconds till impact!" warned Codex from inside.

To the eastern silver skies, five lights shone through.

"Trinity, Phantom-121. I have eyes on. Breaking off."

"Roger that, Phantom-121. Good work."

"Burn in hell," Augustine said as she was swamped in a blinding light.

THE ELDERS

THEMIS, PLANET BOREAS—899 CD

Nightfall blanketed the ice planet's southern hemisphere. Kronos peered out the small-winged spacecraft's frosting window edges at Borea's three beautiful lunar neighbors. The moons radiated off the expansive ice sheets and dark water that stretched in every direction. Kronos sat alone and watched as the autopilot guided the spacecraft toward the elders' home, Themis.

The dark-blue dome was built in 10 CD as a sanctuary for the lawmakers. The solar system's true rulers. From this very rock, galactic law was written and enforced without compromise—even more reason for the future emperor to choose his words carefully.

Ten faint white lights that were evenly spaced formed a circle yards from the dome. The landing pad disappeared from his view as the spacecraft decreased in altitude. Moments later, he felt the vehicle stop in midair and then make its vertical descent. The landing gear lowered, and a thud was heard.

Seconds later, Kronos walked down the lowered ramp. He took a deep breath of iced air, exhaled, and revered the crystal-clear waters that washed against the rocks, supporting Themis.

Two long-brown-haired soldiers, dressed in sandals, black capes, and loincloths, approached from Themis's entrance, which was lit by two torches. Their hands steadied on sheathed and silver swords.

"I request an audience with the elders," said Kronos, listening to the crashing waves and bitter winds that blew his long hair.

"Save yourself the trouble, Your Lordship, and return to Athena. For you have no noble right."

He exhaled a cold fog and said, "Then you leave me no choice."

Kronos used both hands to seize one of the soldiers, preventing him from unsheathing his sword. He booted the second soldier's chest as he charged him. Kronos strong-armed the first soldier and flipped him over onto the ground. The future emperor drew the sword, sweeping the blade across his body. The second soldier dropped his weapon and covered his bleeding throat with two hands. Kronos drove the blade deep into the first soldier's heart, killing him, and threw the sword into the ocean. He left the dead men and proceeded toward Themis's entrance.

He cleared his mind, knowing the elders were studying his every thought. Watching him. When he stood outside the arched wooden Roman door, it opened without physical human intervention. He stepped inside the darkness, and the door creaked closed. A ring of torches encircled the pristine floor. The flames reflected off six arched Roman entrances built over stone hallways.

Kronos came to the circle, took a knee, and lowered his head. His temples began to squeeze, and his forehead burned. Within seconds, he detected the presence of three bodies positioned left, right, and center.

"They've arrived," began the elders all at once in a deep telepathic voice.

"Forgive me, for I deliver a message from my emperor, your humble servant."

The demigods stayed silent. Demigods born from Emperor Lucius Cenaeus's bloodline. The solar system's first emperor.

Before Kronos relayed his next words, the elders said, *"Your emperor acts without rule. His bloodline has destroyed everything we've worked to build. For no man, emperor or servant, shall ever again share in this gift that's been bestowed upon thee. But even you know the Decree is galactic law. For it is written: the elders will not intervene in mortal matters."* They suspected what Kronos was going to ask.

Mortal matters, they say? Whether Athena fell or not, the elders would live only for as long as their masters allowed it. These expired mounds of flesh believed in the preposterousness that they would live to see man's demise and amass unlimited power in their own infallible empire built upon the backs of those conquered. Their minds were mere slaves. Too primitive to understand the true power of the ancient wisdom they sought. Their tongues watered and bodies trilled from having been given a minute taste of what was never to come.

Again, the future emperor was left to defend his stance. *"By the Elder's Decree, I conjure my noble right to regicide."*

"Your emperor is an imbecile to presuppose that pathetic weapon will be of any use. Spare your life and do not concern yourself with such idiocy."

Kronos knew better. *"They're weak and will not survive. I act to preserve the intelligence that you hold so dear and owe your continued existence to."*

"Blasphemous mortal!"

Kronos stayed at peace.

"Remember, it is thee who gives knowledge and can taketh."

"I assure you that I mean no dishonor to you or the Decree. I have seen what they have become—fragments of a failed existence from a forgotten past."

The servants had become the masters, or so the elders believed.

"If my emperor fires the Omega, we will lose this war."

"Are you saying to just give them the GodSphere?"

The battle for Athena was of no concern to the three elders. For they were the almighty puppeteers and would attempt to control the invaders if they colonized the planet and its four sisters, Aquarius, Aphrodisia, Guron-1PC, and even Boreas.

The elders spoke. *"The GodSphere is exactly where it needs to be. Two hundred thousand years of evolution crippled by man. Your speech and intuition are absurd. But by all means, have your quarrel. And when you die, your lordship's bloodline dies with you."*

VOICES

OUTPOST TRINITY, PLANET ATHENA— HEPHAESTUS 32, 899 CD

Knock, knock, knock, knock.

Augustine turned on her side, hoping he'd go away. All she wanted to do was sleep. That was it—just sleep. It had been a couple of days since the battle at Drakon's Rock. She had woken up this morning in the infirmary, disconnected the wires from her veins, and escaped undetected to her tent. The absent sunlight warned her she must've continued sleeping the day away.

Knock, knock.

The stark-naked woman got up to answer the door.

"Can I come in?" asked Codex. He passed by, and she shut the tent's door. "They told us to leave you alone, but I wanted to thank you for what you did out there."

The death toll had to be astronomical. Her survival was a mystery to her. She could barely remember a thing after the missiles destroyed the terraformer. Only a white light. "I was wrong about you, Legionnaire," she said, walking by him. Codex lightly sighed. "You should be gutted and fed to pigs for your insubordination. You nearly cost us the battle." She flipped around and said, "Coward!"

"I understand how things may have appeared."

"Are you telling me that my own eyes and ears have deceived me? That I did not witness you spit in the face of Rome?"

Codex replied, "No, I am not."

Augustine suddenly sat on the bed, leaned over, and ran her fingers through her long hair, leaving one on her forehead. It felt very warm.

"When's the last time you had something to eat?" asked Codex.

"I...I don't recall."

"A couple of doors down, they're throwing a celebration. I know it's a small victory, but it'll help get everyone's spirits up for what comes next."

She was hell-ah-hungry and very horny. She rested her elbows on her knees and looked at Codex. "Why don't I just skip the wine and let you fuck me?"

Codex opened the door.

"Get out!" She grabbed a transmitter and shattered it against the closing door.

THE PALACE, PLANET ATHENA—CRYON 230, 895 CD

From the open master quarters' window, Empress Julia Claudius beheld Helios rise between Utopis's distant skyscrapers. She crossed her wrists on her stomach and exhaled. The ends of her long and dark hair, covered under a black cloak's hood, drifted in the morning winds. The sweat and heat from making love to her husband began to dry on her pale skin.

The empress spent a good part of the 365-Earth-day-long winter caring for her daughter. Teaching her the power of speech and price of freedom. For one day, little Augustine would be off to the Centurion Academy. A day the empress knew she would never bear witness to.

She heard footsteps on the carpet. A set of muscular arms wrapped softly around her hips. She closed her eyes, and when Thaddeus kissed her neck, she opened them again. He pressed his bare cock into her rear end and whispered into her ear, "Do not make this any harder than it has to be."

"Easier said than done," she replied, moving a hand to her backside and fondling him to erection. She slid a finger from his sack's base to the tip, which was laced with cum that she used as lube to gently masturbate him. He expelled warm air on her shoulder and moaned.

"Do you care not for this child?" The emperor gasped and breathed deep. Her hand slid up and down with ease, nursing his shaft. "Or are you not man enough to?" She released his wet dick and attempted to walk away.

The emperor tugged Julia's arm and then backhanded her ass and cursed. "You breathe because I allow it, fucking wench. I swear by the gods, I'll execute you myself."

She spat in his face.

"Guards!" he shouted, licking his lips.

Two legionnaires opened the bedroom door.

"Remove the funk of this whore from my sight. I exercise my noble right to divorce. Gag and chain her to the palace square for all's pleasure. Tell the people...she insisted. She's yours."

As the guards stepped forward, the empress brandished the Crucifier from underneath her cloak. She grasped the lustrous sword's silver grip and gutted the closest legionnaire. She extracted the blade from his intestines and without hesitation swung it to her right, decapitating her final victim. She kept her back to Thaddeus and said, "Let's see if you're a man of your word."

"Urrgh!" She threw the Crucifier's weight around, slicing his eye open, and it clashed on Thaddeus's Drakon Venom. The two met force with force. Eye to bleeding eye, the empress foredoomed, "The last thing you'll feel is my sword boring into the darkness that you call a heart."

Julia suffered an inhuman kick to the stomach, and Thaddeus executed a powerful uppercut to the empress, sending her across the room. Her body broke a standing stone statue of Lucius Cenaeus in half.

She knew deep down that her death would not go unavenged. When the girl discovered her true purpose,

Thaddeus would pay with his life. Julia's hand shivered as she reached for her sword. Reeking of vehemence, she returned to her feet, with her hood lowered. "O thanatos mou tha einai endoxos!" she yelled, running at the naked emperor.

Thaddeus's Drakon Venom swung above the empress's head. She drove the Crucifier into his abdomen. She dug and twisted it deeper. Thick gore topped her dual fists. "Even the emperor bleeds." The emperor's hand encased her throat, and he shot her backward through a closed stained-glass window.

Her bones hammered on icy stone layers that broke her forty-four-foot fall.

Splat!

Empress Claudius was sprawled facedown on snow-covered grass. Her unborn child's genes had altered her own DNA, allowing her to barely survive the deadly fall.

He would seek unchallenged rule throughout the galaxy. Dethrone the elders and declare himself the one true god. She suspected his intentions before the child was born. He would try to stop her from ruling at all costs.

The snow crunched close to her.

She came to her feet, seeing the bare-skinned emperor. Her stomach ached, and the snow under her toes had turned a dark red. She hawked a glob of blood and said, "The gods themselves will kneel before her." He walked forward and assailed the Drakon Venom through Julia's heart. Her lungs and throat filled with fluid, and she choked. Her chin became wet.

"Good-bye, my empress." She heard the sword slide out of her skin.

"Mommy!" cried her daughter. Augustine, covered in a tiny woolen coat and hood, ran from the snowy rose garden. Thaddeus looked at her and raised a claw. The girl fell unconscious, and the empress dropped, succumbing to her wound.

▲ ▲ ▲

OUTPOST TRINITY, PLANET ATHENA— HEPHAESTUS 32, 899 CD

"My lady? My lady!"

The young woman suddenly acknowledged the voice and discovered her hand was cradling a red cup of clear liquid. Soldiers, civilians, and support personnel bumped booties to loud dance music, feasted on various meats, and chugged spirits. The lights were dim inside the room, which smelled heavily of perfumes and sweat.

"You gonna be all right? I know—you need someone to help you back to your tent," said the clean-cut medic, whom she vaguely remembered fighting alongside. The twentysomething black male rubbed her shoulder and said, "Let's get you to bed."

"What's your name, again?" Augustine asked. She felt as if someone had taken a sledgehammer to her noggin. "How did I get here?"

"You *do* need to lie down," he said, smiling. "Yes?"

"Yes, yes, I do. Thank you."

"Hey, Romeo," said Bryana as the man tried leading Augustine from against the wall and across the dance floor.

She and the man turned around, and Bryana knocked the bejesus out of him. The man dropped his drink and was held back by two others.

The sergeant emptied her red cup by tossing the liquid in the medic's face.

"Vag licking—" A crowd had formed.

"Fuck this shit, bro. It ain't worth it. Sergeant's on her side now," said one of his comrades. The three men left.

"Thirsty nigga," said Bryana under her breath. "No offense, but you look like shit. You've been standing against this wall staring into whatever the fuck for ten minutes now. See any pussy you like? Let me know. We can share. But for now"—she took the cup out of Augustine's hand—"how about you give me this, and we get some fresh air?"

Augustine stepped out of the building into a starry sky, with Eon in full view. A cool summer night's current wafted across the outpost.

Augustine began to breathe easily, feeling her sinuses clear. She said, "I don't remember how I got here, but thanks. I need to go for a walk."

"No, it's the least I could do. Look, I'm sorry about what was said. These centurions come along, and…" Bryana shook her head and put a finger to her nose. "I'm sorry." She sniffled.

"Do not mourn the dead. Pick up your sword and avenge them."

"Bryana, what the hell's taking so long! Get your little ass over here," called a man from a group of Phoenix Squad legionnaires.

"You're right." Bryana wiped her tears, turned her head, and screamed, "Fuck off! I'm coming." She said to Augustine, "Why don't you come play cards with us? We stole extra barbecue and some of that rich-folk stuff ya'll drink." She laughed, continuing to wipe her eyes.

"Sarge!"

"Cool your shit!"

"Go enjoy your spoils," Augustine said. "Tomorrow you fight."

"You know, you're all right. See you around." Bryana jogged briefly and then ran and playfully jump kicked the group of guys.

Augustine walked away from the large auditorium, one of the outpost's few solid structures, and looked at the black forest beyond the encampment. She traveled between rows of tents, where legionnaires smoked and rejoiced in victory. She listened to centurions dramatize their parts in the battle to gullible college-age females. Two hookers and their johns, who stood outside the brothel tent, raised beers and cheered. "To the empress!" With her eyes to the ground, Augustine smiled and continued on.

The war was far from over. But the previous day's small victory gave the people hope. Glued them together to achieve greater things. Their defiance against the extraterrestrial threat was an undeniable message to the universe: stay home!

Augustine arrived at a gate in the reinforced barbed wire that'd been recently erected around the outpost. She looked behind her and then to the tower's guard. The gate cranked open. She wasn't surprised he didn't question her motives for leaving unescorted.

She reminisced about the bright light that had cooked her skin at Drakon's Rock. From what she was told by medical staff, she was the only one on her team who had gone unconscious. And that it was a miracle that any of them had survived the impact and were void of a single symptom: blindness, confusion, or various other debilitating injuries.

Augustine's memory of leaving the tent began to return. Codex's refusal to lie with her had almost made her order his execution. She debated staying in the tent, but the smell of sizzled drakon's meat, salted hog's fat, vegetables, pudding, and freshly picked berries was too delicious to pass up. She sat at the head table, had her fixings, poured two stiff ones, and...

It had been nearly four Athena years since she'd seen her mother. So long ago that her dreams, and now daydreams, distorted their last moments together. But this time, the memory felt more alive. Lucid, even. As though she were there to witness the empress's merciless execution at the emperor's hand. Her mind pitilessly splintered to oblivion, and then there was darkness.

Augustine traveled by way of a full moon and the galaxy's purple nebula millions of miles away. She learned that since the terraformer had been destroyed, Athena's atmosphere had wasted little time reconfiguring itself to its previous state: bright summer days followed by mild to algid nights encapsulated in trillions of stars. She walked on moist leaves, choosing one star that stood out among the others. She ruminated over how a species so advanced could harbor so much hate and such little regard for life. *Is there a way to destroy them completely? They value us as nothing more than a spreading plague in an otherwise undisturbed solar system.* She'd caught wind that Sentinel had tagged the invaders the *Dr'og*. The extraterrestrials had colonized all of Utopis's central region for some unknown cause. The region was ten times as fortified as Drakon's Rock. It would take thousands upon thousands of soldiers to infiltrate the city. If it came to it, she'd be among her men charging into battle. But for now, small units conducted search-and-rescue missions for civilians. Salvaged and convoyed supplies to decentralized colonies. The emperor's forces were wearing thin, as well as their fortitude. She started to envision an arid world controlled by the Dr'og. Millions of enslaved humans laboring to death, building unimaginable technological structures. Forced to procreate, and the weak used as sustenance. *Like hell they will.*

Augustine rubbed her bare arms and could see her breath. She was starting to turn back when a tree branch cracked. She stopped and looked left. An unseen creature gurgled, and she heard what sounded like a large wing flap.

Augustine's mind squeezed. She gasped.

A mystical force guided her deeper into the wood line to a fallen tree. Fear escaped her, though she knew to run.

He won't hurt you, but they will.

"Who said that!" Her voice echoed in the cold darkness. She took two steps back from the injured drakon that was lying on its stomach.

As the beast cowered, a large object bashed the back of Augustine's shoulders, causing her to slump facedown. She spit through gnashed teeth. Footsteps crushed fallen twigs.

"Loose bitch. Think you can show me up just 'cause you got money?" cursed the medic. A gym shoe crossed her face and busted her nose. His hand forced her neck down, grinding her face in the mud.

Male voices laughed, and a bottle was smashed.

His warm breath smelled of alcohol. "This shit ain't for us no more. The world is fucked! You are fucked! Tired of little musty cunts like you coming along and fucking shit up. So I decided to check out. But before I go, I decided to pay my respects to the throne."

They dragged her by the ankles, and she clawed at the ground, screaming.

"What's with all the fuss, huh? Damn tease. You ain't shit, ugly, fat bitch. I learned a long time ago that your kind ain't nothing but a bunch of privileged cock-hungry hoes out to take advantages of guys like me. The ones who work hard. Like you too good or some shit. It's what gets you off. Am I right?"

Two others turned her over and pinned her wrists to the ground. "Aggh!"

"So I got really fucking tired of playing the nice guy. I figured, if they can do it, I can do it. Wouldn't you say that's a fair assumption"—he put a hand over his heart and mocked in an uppity voice—"my lady?"

The medic undid his zipper and pissed in Augustine's bloody face while drinking a bottle of beer. "Now, you haven't gone and caught yourself an STD from all those trains you been running, has you? We all saw him come out of the tent. And we all know you been sucking his dick."

"Motherfucker!" she badgered. Another thug held her ankles. Her waist spasmed on the ground as she tried to breach the pin.

"I'm gonna teach you the meaning of sharing. Here's the first lesson, bitch: I'm going in yo shit raw." Her forehead was split open, and glass sprinkled her brow. The medic sported an erection through his blue jeans, and he got down on both knees over her chest. He scooted his swinging cock next to her chin and jerked it. He popped his dick on her perched lips and cheeks. "Open your mouth." His hand left smack on her right cheek. "I said, open up!"

"Aggh!"

The voice returned. "You disappoint me. You're stronger than this. Now, prove it."

The medic alternated hands, slapping across her saturated face.

"Fuck it, man. Let's just kill her," said his bud.

"No! I came for some neck, and I'm not leaving until—"

A body tackled the medic to the ground. His boys released the emperor's daughter and went after her rescuer. "Run! Get out of here!" said Codex.

Channel your hate. Make them pay for what they've done. Keeping her head down, Augustine moved to two knees and put her hands on them. Her temples throbbed. "Aggh!"

Punches were thrown and landed.

Augustine rose with lava brewing in her heart. Her eyes started to sting. A torrid liquid hastened through her veins until her fists were covered in flames.

Do it.

Free of pain, she ran and drilled a fist into a thug's chest. She squeezed his beating heart and ripped it from its smoking cavity. The man's eyes turned white, and he slunk. The others left Codex and frantically backed up. Augustine extended both hands and doused two men in fire. Their dying screams pleased her. In her peripheral, Codex trotted and stayed near a tree. Burning bodies surrounded the medic.

Show no mercy.

Augustine drove her fiery fist into the soil. A line of red flames caught up to and fried him alive. She grimaced as the blazing body danced uncontrollably. The flames intensified, and his skin peeled to bone.

She dropped with her legs folded under her. Each breath was deep and sporadic. Her hands felt numb. She saw a caped figure lie in wait behind the flames, which lit his young face and long white hair. He came forth.

"Kronos," she managed to say.

"Augustine. It's been a while."

The drakon flapped its wing.

Codex rushed to her side, knelt, and to Kronos said, "I don't know what the fuck is going on here, but back off!"

Kronos parted his cloak, holding out his gloved palms face up. He stroked Codex's cheek and said, "Mortal fool, do you not recognize God when you see her? Sleep."

Codex slumped unconscious.

"What did you…do to me?" asked Augustine.

His dark cape closed over his front half. The Lord's eyes were pitch white. "Every generation of your bloodline has grown stronger and stronger, leading up to this very moment."

"What…are you talking about?" She continued to heave and then remembered Meegan's dying words about her father. The girl had taken her secrets to the grave. She looked up and said, "Your daughter—"

"Is dead. However, you are very much alive. Evolution, my empress. Our visitors are not here by chance. They seek what your father has denied us—infinite power. The GodSphere."

She coughed. "God—wha?"

Kronos said, "I'm sure you've learned in your studies about the accident on Guron-1PC. But I assure you, that was no accident."

She remembered reading that a disturbed miner had committed suicide, causing the site to collapse. The first incident of its kind since syncorium mining operations had begun in 7 CD.

Devil's Wings sounded nearby.

"I have so much to teach you." The Lord waved a claw, and Augustine's world turned black.

FUCKED IN MORE WAYS THAN ONE

OUTPOST TRINITY, PLANET ATHENA— HEPHAESTUS 33, 899 CD

"Last time, Darius. Where is she?" said First Centurion Vlad Hexgrm. "And don't give me that Dr'og-attacked-us story line again, because I've had enough of it."

CSMg Ariel Lucas leaned her back against the wall behind Hexgrm's desk. Her left shoulder rested on a tall grandfather clock. Codex centered on the swaying disk inside the glass.

"Four legionnaires burned alive. Beer bottles everywhere. We had to put the poor drakon down that got shot with your personal hunting rifle. Let me tell you what I think happened. Correct me if I'm wrong, but just hear me out. We got us five strong males and a teenage girl who went on a little camping trip without our permission. Got our lady drunk, did some drakon hunting, and, in the mist of it all, ended up shooting themselves and lighting one another on fire. One of ya got scared and buried her body, and I'm going on a whim and saying it was you, seeing you're the only one still alive. Or even fed it to the damn drakon, for all I know. Will you just reason with me here? I can only do so much; the emperor has the last word. The least I can do is recommend a crucifixion."

Codex finally faced Hexgrm's middle-aged mug and high-and-tight haircut. The stocky and broad-shouldered officer was soft compared to a lot of his fellow centurions.

"OK, Master Legionnaire—if I can even call you that anymore. Have it your way." He signaled for two legionnaires who held the tent entrance.

"Wait a minute," said Ariel. She nodded for both legionnaires to step outside, and they complied. "Darius, I'm going to give you the benefit of the doubt. Our Lady's behavior has been somewhat of a challenge since her arrival. And I wouldn't be surprised if she disappeared on her own, given that we searched under every rock for her."

Codex breathed easily.

"However, I see no reason to imprison this man. After all, it was his squad that brought down the terraformer. Sir, would it bother you to give us a moment alone?"

Hexgrm lifted his hands, leaned back in his chair, and placed them back on the desk. He got up and left.

Once the tent door closed, she came from around the desk and perched her hot ass on its corner with her legs crossed. She then spread her thighs and said, "Seeing that you're under my command, we'll discuss your limitations in private."

Codex squeezed his fist and popped up. As he approached the door, Ariel said, "I'm most confident that we'll find a way to reason with each other."

Shortly thereafter, Codex projected his anger into a punching bag. Left, right, left, right. "Rrrgh!" he yelled, punching it one last time and then catching the bag as it swung back.

Bryana, who was squatting, racked the bar and walked over. "You OK? I know this ain't the place, but she had us all fooled. Little bitch up and fucked us all over. I heard they wanna talk to everyone."

Codex struck the bag and left it swinging. He scooped up his gym bag, unfastened his weightlifting gloves, and clutched them in one hand. He fisted open the main entrance. He listened to it close and open again.

"What happened out there? I think I deserve to know. We all do. Ever since the last mission, you've acted like a damn recluse. What aren't you telling me?"

He paced it to the new unisex cadillac. Emperor Claudius had ordered all outposts to undergo refortifications. In only a few days, Trinity had transformed from a bare base to a sustainable military installation. The civil engineering legion had busted their asses nonstop building new facilities, sleeping quarters for military and civilians, and everything else they would need for the long haul and inescapable glacial freeze—Cryon.

Codex accessed the surprisingly empty cadillac and threw his gym bag on a wooden bench. He addressed Bryana in a low pitch. "Shit that I don't want any part of, and neither would you. Something big is happening, and the empire is doing their damnedest to keep it a secret."

Bryana's eyes turned away.

"I have enough shit on my plate," he said, taking off his black tank top.

"What's the secret? The cat's out the bag, if you haven't noticed. We've been raided by extraterrestrials from who knows what planet. I don't think there's much else to hide, even if they knew about the Dr'og."

"Didn't you see what happened at Drakon's Rock? Feel it? You and I should both be toe tagged and bagged. But somehow, we survived. Now, I can't explain it, but"—he watched the door to make sure no one entered—"forget it."

Bryana frowned slightly. "I'm not sure if you knew, but Sentinel found something at the site of impact."

Codex unlaced his boots and plopped them off. He lost his pants, and they fell to his ankles.

Bryana pulled her personal transmitter out of her sweat shorts' pocket. She pressed a few digital buttons and rotated the device's face. "I have a friend who works intelligence. Sent me these this morning."

A stint in the Citadel would be the least of Bryana's worries if intelligence knew she received classified information without authorization.

"What am I looking at?"

"Look closer," she replied, enlarging the on-screen image.

The space-guided missiles toppled much of the caverns and surrounding rock formations. The aliens' octagon-shaped terraformer was reduced to metallic scraps. Sentinel sent hordes of men to comb through the wreckage for Dr'og weapons and technology. Possibly to reverse engineer it and use it against them. He noticed that there were four avenues of approach: west, north, east, and south. Between each compass direction were the cliffs used by the support teams, with the exception of the cliffs at the northwest and northeast directions. The entire layout looked like a giant X missing the center, where the terraformer had hovered. But where the ascending cliffs once stood were massive metallic ramps. The terraformer was superseded by a dome-like structure that appeared to have been buried underground.

The cadillac door opened, and two sweaty female legionnaires found shower stalls, demanding Bryana's attention. She turned off the transmitter and slid it in her pocket.

She kept her voice to a minimum. "That rock is more than seven million Earth years old. Whatever that thing is, it sure didn't come from us. My friend's saying the Dr'og are roughly on the same technological level as us. Give or take a couple of thousand years, but he believes it was built by a third civilization."

Codex made sure he heard running shower water before asking, "What is the order throwing at the people?"

"Anything that'll keep them focused on the Dr'og. Somehow, they built it under our noses—the same brain-dead gullible shit."

"Get rid of it."

"Yes, sir."

Codex stepped into an empty shower stall, pulling the curtain halfway. He watched Bryana leave.

After sundown, he knocked once on Ariel's personal bunker. He sneaked his finger inside his black military cargo pants' pocket. The collar of a black Sentinel-embroidered jean jacket touched his earlobes. He took these precautions even though Ariel's bunker was well off from tent city, where he chose to sleep over the new single-level dorms.

He gave it another try and then immediately turned around. At least he could be honest and say he stopped by.

The door opened, and he stopped moving. His head lifted to the sky, and he exhaled cold air at Eon. Whatever perfume she was wearing could gag a whole platoon.

"Come in before you catch a death of a cold."

Codex faced the music. He lowered his head and went inside.

"Dinner? A cup of bourbon? Smoke?"

He kept his reserve the best he could and said, "I'll pass." His animal instincts came alive, seeing her breast blossoming through a strained military-grade black shirt. Her ass and long black hair led him into a decorated wooden kitchen, where she picked up a bottle and poured its contents into two cups. Roasted suckling pig meat, porridge, and vegetables were prepared on the table.

"Don't be so damn uptight, Master Legionnaire," said Ariel, sipping at her whiskey. She moved inches away from his face. "Drink. That's an order." She humphed and downed more.

Codex expelled air through his nostrils and then emptied the cup.

"Good boy," said his leader. "Have another."

His cup dipped from the bottle's weight. She drank from the bottle before pouring more for herself.

The master legionnaire stopped fighting his feelings and quietly admitted that having Augustine come on to him had him hot for Ariel, who was the most beautiful woman he'd ever seen. He had majored in ancient Earth cultures and perceived that Ariel came from an Arabic lineage. Egyptian, to be approximate.

Codex didn't waste another second. "I mean to be of no rush. I am curious as to the limitations that you'll impose on me." He finished the second glass, and she refilled it again.

"Good. So I have all night to figure what it is I want to do with you." Ariel sucked down more alcohol out of the bottle. She rested her forearms on his shoulders, keeping the bottle in one hand. "Is there a Mrs. Codex I am unaware of?"

He pictured his mixed wife's curly brown hair and reminisced over her comforting embrace. Her soft caress and warm lips. The affection that coddled his soul from when they made love. He swallowed. "My wife and son are missing."

Ariel made an aloof and pouty face. "I'm so sad to hear that. I'm sure she'll turn up." The woman came in a tad bit closer. Her lips nearly brushed his. "This minor inconvenience shouldn't stop you from taking care of your...needs."

His cock twitched against her crotch.

She pecked his lips. "We all have needs"—kiss—"don't we?" Her red lips captured his. She jumped up, and Codex caught her, allowing the woman to wrap her legs around his hips. The bottle dropped, and he pushed her back to the kitchen wall.

"Ooh." She gasped as he licked her rose-scented neck. He let her down, and she undid his zipper.

His eyes remained closed, feeling her cottonlike fist take him into her mouth. He opened them to watch Ariel's see-sawing head. Codex looked at the ceiling, fantasizing about Augustine. He had been a fool not to have sex with her. Her young body and enticing eyes. He wanted her so badly, but the code he'd sworn to uphold stopped him from dishonoring it.

He panted, sensing Ariel's soggy tongue wag and do tricks on his dick. She nursed his cum sack and jerked him off. A deep breath escaped his lungs when Ariel stuffed his bulging cock to the back of her throat.

How he wished this were Augustine swallowing and sucking on him.

Ariel put two hands on his hips and used just her mouth, rotating her head. She nuzzled him deep once more but gagged, and he watched spit leak out of her mouth. Ariel used her tongue to tickle his shaft on the way out. She got up and turned around.

His lust imprisoned him as he undid her cargo pants and underwear. He buried his slick rod into her warm and welcoming snatch. Ariel put both hands on the kitchen wall while Codex rammed his cock into his commander with no shame.

"Fuck me! Yeah, fuck this pussy hard, baby. Fuck it! Harder—that's an order," she moaned. Her head dropped.

Codex's crotch banged against hot ass cheeks, and his cock pleaded to jizz in Ariel's loose but sweet hole. He closed his eyes and imagined the emperor's daughter bent over.

Why don't I just skip the wine and let you fuck me? Why don't I just skip the wine and let you fuck me? Fuck me, fuck me. He played her authoritative and alluring words repeatedly. *Why don't I just skip the wine and let you fuck me?*

"Yes, Aug…Augustine. I want you. Oh, my lady. Augustine. I'm your slave. Punish me. Do what you will."

He grunted, and Ariel pulled him out to get back on her knees. She jacked his dick until blast after blast of cream soiled her sweaty light-brown face and lips. The whore crammed Codex into her mouth, draining what was left over from his chock-full orgasm. He stayed in her mouth and became flaccid. Ariel took him out, got up, and stepped out of her pants. She lifted her shirt and loosened her sports bra. The naked woman walked in the direction of her bathroom and said, "Stay awhile, and we'll discuss my decision over breakfast."

"Fuck," murmured Codex, guilty he'd betrayed his vows.

▲   ▲   ▲

OUTPOST TRINITY, PLANET ATHENA— HEPHAESTUS 34, 899 CD

The bedroom was dark when he awoke. He kept his head on the pillow and rested a forearm on it. The potent alcohol and sin of cheating on his missing wife, Patricia, hung over him like an obsidian cloud that flooded him in his own shit. He rose momentarily and came back down after noticing Ariel was absent. He closed his eyes and prayed that the sex was all she wanted. And that she'd forget about the incident, if he kept silent about being seduced. War turned people into lunatics crazed for fraternizing sex, murder, and other vices—adultery in his case. The invasion had gotten the best of him—hopefully, just this one time.

The bedroom door and his eyes opened. She whistled. "Suit up, lover boy." Ariel turned on the light, burning his irises. He covered the ceiling light with a hand and moved upward to brace his spine against the headboard. Codex caught his balled-up belongings. "You and the other meatheads are shipping out to Inferno."

Codex dragged out of bed and put on his pants, watching a fully uniformed Ariel drink coffee.

"Against my recommendation, Hexgrm forwarded your case to Thaddeus. However, he squashed it. Shows how much he cares for that little tramp you've grown attached to. Lucky you. He sent this back." Ariel used her transmitter to show Codex two high-value targets (HVTs). "Matthew and Caroline Graesen."

"The old man died off planet years ago."

"Apparently not, if the emperor has ordered his arrest."

This made absolutely no sense. The image of Matt was old. It showed him still in his thirties.

"The old hag's your lead. She's showed face more than once and goes off satellite. She's expendable, but Matthew is to be captured and transported to the Citadel."

Codex finished lacing his combat boots and slipped into his shirt. "The Dr'og?"

"The good thing about Inferno's unruly population is that they know how to fight. We didn't waste much more than a handful of troops to reinforce their numbers. Ironically, the ones we deployed were, as expected, killed by *friendly* fire. On the other hand, the Dr'og, in the last twenty-four hours, have decreased their numbers around the city to almost zero. We've pulled back the GAF and deployed them to Utopis."

"And what makes you think Matt's hiding in Inferno?"

"I don't think, and frankly, I don't give a shit. But these are your orders, and I only get paid to make sure you follow them."

Whether the nobles liked it or not, Inferno was one of the last standing cities on the planet. Outposts and loose refugee pockets harbored what was left of Athena's human population.

"Ready your team. I want you on the ground at zero one hundred hours."

She was crazy as hell if she thought he was taking Phoenix Squad with them. "Since you had your way"—*with me, more than once*, he thought—"how about you leave them out of this? They're support troops. I almost lost a quarter of my team saving Augustine."

"Making love is a two-way street, Hercules." She giggled naughtily. "Don't tell me you didn't enjoy it."

Ariel was ignorant to every word he had said. Codex threw his jacket over a shoulder and said, "I make love to my wife," while starting to pass Ariel.

The libidinous bitch blocked his path with her coconut-scented body. Her long and straight black hair was fashioned out of regulation and prepped for a night out. She savored a dab of almond-spiced coffee and then said, "Why, she must've been one satisfied dame. Did you think of Patricia when you moaned the girl's name?"

Ariel's eyes enlarged, and the coffee cup shattered on the floor. Pictures and toiletries fell off the dresser. Codex's grip kept the wench's head and shoulder blades fast against the wall.

"Do not *ever* speak of her. Are we clear?"

Her eyes went haywire.

Codex released his hold, and Ariel panted. He left the bedroom and said, "I'll see you at debrief."

Raining Fire

Underground Battle Station, Planet Athena—Hephaestus 34, 899 CD

The emperor watched violent armed conflict on the screens inside the underground battle station (UBS). He remained in the room's center, studying the holographic war board. Various regions were covered in red, indicating complete Dr'og control. Inferno and a handful of other cities would fall if he did not act.

"Sir, incoming report from First Centurion Juno at Drakon's Rock. Would you like me to patch him through?" asked a legionnaire at the controls.

The emperor nodded. A negroid centurion's face covered all the screens, showing a single image.

"Report," ordered Thaddeus.

"My Emperor, we've nearly completed digging into the site of impact, and what we've found is…quite alarming."

The emperor did not speak, so Juno continued the report.

"The structure underneath the rock is intelligently designed. The technology is more complex than anything I've come across. I don't know what to make of any of it. We're leaning toward a power transistor used to control the planet's energy, or a maybe a weapon."

He said to the controllers, "If you will."

A body camera replaced the centurion's face. Thaddeus saw the inside of a shaking shuttle and its two pilots. Armed legionnaires, who were harnessed, stood up and held the ceiling rails. Thaddeus heard a thunderous bump and a hiss from the shuttle coming to a standstill. The rear hatch opened, and Juno, along with the legionnaires, hurried down the ramp.

Thaddeus saw a red dome structure made of glass and a small staircase underneath it. He listened to the intelligence officer's heavy breathing.

"Let me get a bit clos…" Juno mumbled, jogging up to the dome. The glass was lit at dusk by syncorium-powered towers. Light waves rushed through the dome with each movement of the camera. "That's not all. Now we're on to the real kicker."

The legionnaires trained their weapons at the head of the staircase that led into the dome. Thaddeus could hear the centurion unsheathing his sword. He ascended the staircase into an extremely dark room. He turned on his galea's affixed flashlight and slowly turned his head across the room until it came to a tall chair that was encircled by a thin sheet of glass. Juno's breathing deepened. He crept around the chair and the battle station and gasped in horror. A scrawny gray creature, absent a visible mouth, lay presumably dead in the chair. Its eyes were closed, and its arms were slumped on either side. Juno turned around and broadcasted his legionnaires examining the dome's floor. Their helmet lights reflected off unclothed bodies, causing the observers to jump a second time. Along the walls were assumed holographic workstations, given that only sheets of glass were supported by vertical metallic bases. "Twenty, maybe more, of these beings are in here. No telling how long they've been down here. Not a single sign of decomposition."

"Fuck!" cursed a legionnaire, discharging his rifle.

"Hold your fire!" said Juno. The camera followed him.

"Fucking thing just moved. I swear it…it, it looked at me, and…"

Black blood poured from the alien's fresh chest wound.

"Has the area been sealed?" asked Thaddeus.

"Certainly, My Emperor."

"Who else knows about the bodies?"

"Information's on a need-to-know basis."

"By my order, place the area under strict Sentinel intelligence control indefinitely."

"Roger that."

A millennium of dark knowledge was on the verge of revelation to unworthy and ignorant peasants. They needed to be eradicated, and the Dr'og needed to be stopped. Thaddeus addressed his legionnaires. "Are we ready to launch?"

"Affirmative, My Emperor. Omega stands at one hundred percent."

Their fate was a testament to his empirical power.

"Fire."

▲   ▲   ▲

MOUNT PANTHEON, PLANET ATHENA— HEPHAESTUS 34, 899 CD

Strong and chilling winds crisscrossed her body. Her eyes struggled to open, and she faced a dark-orange sun that was setting behind mountain peaks, which were flush with the ocean's horizon. Her hand touched rock, and she tasted dirt as she heaved herself off her side. Darkened clouds traversed the azure sky, and her brunette hair swirled as she came to a knee. She remembered the man who stood at the mountain's edge with his cape and flowing white hair, turned away from her. He then faced her, with his back toward Helios and his cloak covering his armor.

"Infinite power is what the gods have bestowed upon you."

She was now on both feet.

"Lead us, Augustine. All my life, I've practiced mastering only a fraction of what you do so easily."

"I...I don't know what you're talking about."

"I showed you the truth about your mother's death. Before, you were far too young to understand what was happening. As patriotic as she was, she died trying to kill your father, whose bloodline drank of the forbidden...fruit."

"What did this to me? How did I become like this?" asked Augustine, looking at her palms and expecting them to become aflame.

"Not what but who. The Ereb, a civilization that witnessed its own destruction, as an inevitable result of their own greed."

Augustine's stomach bubbled, and she let loose. She wiped her lips, keeping both hands propped on her knees.

"Beneath Athena, the remnants of what was once the most powerful species in the observable universe breathe and thrive but only in the frailest of forms. They've spent the last several thousand years resurrecting their society from ashes."

"I don't give a shit," she said before spewing more gunk on the dirt. All her life, she'd known Kronos to tell the truth. And this time, she was sure, was no different. If this was the case, humankind was in the middle of a war for—

She said, "This GodSphere. What is it, and how do we destroy it?" There'd be no other way to save the empire than to remove this device of extraterrestrial origin.

Kronos made two small steps toward Augustine, managing to keep his cloak wrapped around his body. "Every planet holds a GodSphere—the first and last element of life. Intelligent species use it to fuel their planet and technology, but there have been countless civilizations that have perished in their attempts to replicate it. The Ereb fed off this element, harnessing vast powers beyond our comprehension. Why destroy the very dust that created"—his hand stroked her face—"this beautiful specimen that stands before me?"

Augustine shoved Kronos's hand away. "Are you fucking blind?" she snarled. "Look at what it's done to my people. My friends. Your daughter. There's an asinine number of untouched planets. Why us? If the Ereb destroyed themselves, why are the Dr'og here?"

Augustine gazed into the twilight at not one but no fewer than fourteen descending starry lights. The lights began to branch off, aiming for separate areas. They were tailed by more. "Fool!" said Kronos, watching the lights. "I'm afraid I'm too late."

"What's happening?" she asked, holding her stomach and walking to the mountain edge.

"Extinction. Come, we must hurry!" said Kronos as a blazing light descended upon them. He consulted his SpecNav and inputted a code.

Augustine's knees weakened, and she fell over from an eruption at the mountain's base. Kronos stumbled slightly but managed to reach and pull her up. Another missile crashed against the mountain, only this time the impact felt much closer. Kronos blanketed Augustine under his cloak, shielding her from shrapnel. A quad starburner, V-winged VTOL came shooting out the dark-red clouds. "This way!" said Kronos, leading the sprint toward the mountaintop's far side. Augustine tripped slightly but kept her footing by blocking her fall with her hand.

Fire and brimstone rained on Athena. Only her father could order a scorched-Athena policy. If he could not have it, no one could.

The spacecraft's pilot weaved and dodged the smoldering missiles and then hovered the craft on the mountaintop. The side door slid up, and Kronos stopped to look back. Augustine jumped and caught the edge with her midtorso. She dangled a bit before pushing herself up, using both hands. She took Kronos's extended hand and yanked him aboard.

"Strap yourselves down and hang tight!" said the negroid pilot. The space vehicle was outfitted with six seats, two on each side behind the pilot and copilot chairs. Augustine quickly harnessed herself in, and Kronos followed.

"Why would he do this?"

The Omega had turned the sky blood red. The sight of it boiled her blood. Her feet vibrated on the steel floorboard. A Dr'og spacecraft no more than three hundred yards ahead cracked apart. Its flaming metal dropped out of the sky.

"Yeah!" shouted the pilot. "That ought to show those motherfuckers! Who's the boss now, bitch? Who's the boss?"

She looked at Kronos's slanted brows. She sensed the hate brewing in him—the same hate she felt for her father, who'd brought hell on Athena.

The pilot engaged the four starburners, and Augustine witnessed the interior turn 180 as he jetted them into outer space.

I Run This Bitch!

Inferno, Planet
Athena—Hephaestus 35, 899 CD

"Well, I'll be damned," said Bulldog, the Devil's Wing pilot, to the master legionnaire and wingman, Bryana. "I wish you guys could see this. Half the damn city looks like it's been destroyed."

Codex looked at Bryana through his black helmet's visor. Her black muscle cuirass was tight around her abdomen. She held the full automatic with her finger outside the trigger guard. He had debated bringing the young girl along, but her determination to avenge her family's death would prove beneficial when the time was right. He knew that behind her visor was a mouth salivating for alien blood.

The emperor wanted Matt, and Codex wanted answers. He was chasing a ghost believed to have been long dead.

From what he knew, the Omega fired from Athena's moon had wiped out nearly half the planet's cities. If Matt *had* in fact been alive, chances were he had perished or was now clinging to life. This thought brought to mind his wife and child. He feared Patricia and his son, Izaiah, had been killed. Sure, he would deliver the emperor his man, but with him would come a bullet. He held no reservations about ending the emperor's life and was prepared for the lethal consequences. His chest started to rise, and he increased the pressure around his rifle's handgrip.

Bulldog opened the circular exit chute on the cargo bay's floor. The Devil's Wing rested in midair, twenty feet above ground. Codex jumped through the hole and used his gauntlets' depressurizing system to break the fall. He heard Bryana's overhead when he landed.

The Devil's Wing ascended. Bulldog's task was to stay within range of the legionnaires so Codex could use the ship's technology as a boosting signal for his SpecNav to connect with Sentinel's satellites. He would stay airborne until mission evac.

Bodies everywhere. Nothing but pieces of human and Dr'og. Makeshift homes smoked, and trash blew about in the winds.

The emperor will answer for this. To take the lives of his own people was no way to win a war. The sacrifice of the innocent was a diabolical decision only the vilest of men could carry out.

"So where do we start?" Bryana asked Codex, who started to walk up the dusty roadway.

Codex half turned and dipped his neck in the direction he was going.

Two green humanoid outlines were huddled near a desecrated building's corner wall. The larger of the two picked up the smaller one and quickstepped it around the building. The mother had a right to fear Sentinel. Codex and Bryana were walking targets for any loose gun. Negotiating for their lives was no longer an option. The emperor's ruthlessness had severed any strategic alliance that may have been formed between Inferno and Sentinel.

"Help me!" sobbed an unseen voice. "Help me, please. Someone, I beg of you. Aggh!"

"No," said Codex.

Bryana slowed her pace in the voice's direction.

The man's screams turned into a gurgle.

"One o'clock," warned Codex.

He and Bryana sprinted behind the building and then to the farthest edge. She took the rear as Codex observed a machete-wielding, dreadlocked negro yank an unhelmeted legionnaire out of a thrashed store by the neck, using a noose. He was surrounded by two men armed with Dr'og weapons. A swarm of gun-toting men and women appeared out of the flickering darkness.

The presumed leader spoke. "Get this muthafucka up."

His men obeyed and brought the man to his knees. The leader took a baseball stance and rested the blade's sharp edge on the side of the legionnaire's neck.

"We have to stop them," said Bryana.

Codex didn't reply. He watched the scene play out.

A female soldier cried, being pulled by her hair before the leader. Her sweaty and bare breasts jiggled, and her hands fought with the man's undeniably strong grip. The woman was flung forward onto her stomach.

"We can't let him kill them," said Bryana.

Codex put up two fingers to silence his partner's pleas.

The leader drove his boot into the woman's spine. "Shut up, bitch! This is my city. You got that? Didn't no one tell yo funky ass to come down here?" The man waved his free hand toward the spotty flames about the streets. "You see this? This shit is yo fault."

Whack, whack, whack. The woman screamed bloody murder as the machete slashed against her shoulder blades. The next *whack* caused her head to roll.

He walked over to the remaining prisoner. "I'm in a giving mood today." He pointed the machete at the man. "You go back and tell dat nigga, Thaddeus, Inferno's ours." His followers hooted and pumped their rifles into the night sky.

A man untied the noose, brought the legionnaire up, and stomp kicked him in the ass. The victim ran the way Codex and Bryana had come from.

"We're taking a shortcut," said Codex. "That's our guy."

One of the men discharged a small automatic pistol in the air and wolf called. The dreadlocked man entered the back seat of a nearby four-door rover that was absent a roof. His comrades hopped into separate vehicles of similar make and model.

Codex fired a tracking device that latched onto the leader's trunk and monitored his SpecNav. "Tracking," he read.

Codex and Bryana walked back to the rear of the building, where they came face-to-face with a golden-haired woman and child. The lady brought the girl in closer. "We're not here for you. Who is he?" asked Codex.

The woman stepped herself and the child back. Codex put out his arm to block Bryana's advance. "What's your name?"

"Miriam."

"I'm Jezebel," said the girl.

"Hush!" exclaimed her mother.

He saw the purple bruises on Miriam's face and legs. Jezebel's legs were toothpicks. Codex unsheathed a blade from his boot. He reversed the handle at Miriam.

She took the weapon and said, "They call him Shogun."

"Sounds fitting." He maximized a 3-D image from his SpecNav of Matthew and Caroline Graesen. "Do these two faces look familiar?"

Miriam grabbed the bug-eyed girl's arm and tried walking away. "Leave us. We want no trouble."

Bryana blocked her path, leaving her weapon in Weaver ready.

"I want to know where this Shogun lays his head at night."

Miriam's eyes zigzagged left and right. "They'll rape the both of us for talking to you. But if you must know, five miles east. Can't miss it. Only a damn fool enters there. Now, leave us."

"Can we trust her?" asked Bryana through her helmet's internal mouthpiece, after muting the external speaker.

Codex did the same. "We'll find out."

She treaded to the left so Miriam and Jezebel could pass.

He powered up a 3-D image of Shogun's tracker from his SpecNav and noticed the hologram flicker.

"Bulldog, Phoenix lead, come in," Codex transmitted to the Devil's Wing.

"Bulldog."

"I'm running into a bit of interference. Are you picking up anything?"

"Yeah. I'm clear on this end, sir. Increasing SAT signal and dropping coordinates for ten miles east. The Temple of Jupiter."

The hologram cleared up, and Codex minimized it. "We keep to the shadows."

▲　▲　▲

PLANET APHRODISIA—899 CD

The spacecraft Augustine and Kronos had been traveling in decelerated out of dark speed—the fastest humans could travel using dark matter. The Roman Empire's discovery of dark matter's capabilities in AD 1912 had set the stage for space travel and the development of ungodly weapons.

Since leaving Athena, she felt half awake and as though she were suffering from extreme depersonalization. She watched herself escape the descending horror that had lit fire to her home world. Her chest was heavy, and each time she rested her head on the chair, vertigo set in. The sun glared off the cabin window as the spacecraft veered left. She lifted her head slightly. She had only heard stories of this planet, and for the first time, she laid her virgin eyes on its sheer beauty.

Aphrodisia was home to various reptilian species called homosaurs, who mirrored the Earth's extinct dinosaurs. But one particular species, some thousands of years ago, began to walk upright. Their mannerisms were that of early man, but Sentinel refused to classify them as intelligent, due to their not having discovered the element of fire. A now-deceased emperor, whose name escaped her recollection, placed the planet under discreet scientific observation and forbade interference in the homosaurs' evolution.

So why did he bring me here? She believed this was a rhetorical question until Kronos looked at her and smiled from the adjacent chair.

The pilot swooped into Aphrodisia's atmosphere. Her mouth opened at a sparkling waterfall that looked fresher than anything she'd ever sipped. The expanding and tall grassy plains and trees flowed in the warm winds that she couldn't wait to wash over her body. Her veins filled with bliss as she watched small beasts race across the fields. The larger ones walked in threes and fours at a much slower but even pace. A flock of giant winged reptiles flapped in a V-shaped formation.

No war, no unnecessary death, no pillaging for resources. This was life in pure serenity. She touched her left breast and noticed Kronos's smirk.

The pilot flew over a luscious mountain valley split by the bluest of rivers. As he made his descent, her breath expelled when she saw the blue flowers and tall pines decorating the landscape. He began to circle around a large two-story cabin with smoke emitting from its chimney. Wooden slave and soldier quarters were built on each side. The spacecraft became suspended and decreased in altitude.

Augustine waited for the landing gear to secure and unlatched her harness. She got up and went to the side of the craft and waited for the pilot to open the door. Kronos joined her as the door slid open. She closed her eyes and took a deep breath, feeling the sun on her face and smell of fresh flowers carried by the winds.

Kronos jumped down into the grass. His cape spread, and he lifted his head at Helios's comforting temperatures. She assumed this was what scientists called spring, though she had never experienced it. She hesitated to depart the spacecraft for fear she'd infect this tranquil world.

Kronos said, without facing her, "It's OK. It doesn't bite."

She jumped down, and the pilot immediately closed the door. Augustine took a few steps toward Kronos and turned to witness the spacecraft ascend. The landing gear retracted, and the pilot blasted toward space.

She was now stranded on an unfamiliar world with an even more mysterious man. Kronos removed his black cloak and said, "Welcome to Aphrodisia. Here, I will train you to control the power that flows through your blood."

"Or is it me you want to control?"

Kronos reversed, held out a claw, and shot Augustine backward with lightning. Her face caked up grass.

"Urggh," she grunted. She attempted to regain her composure and stand, but a fist lunged down on her back. "Aggh!" She felt the same electric currents traverse her nervous system. A hand collapsed around her neck. Kronos brought her into the air and delivered blows to Augustine's stomach. A final punch shot her away from him.

"Yes, I've seen what it's done," he said, answering her earlier question on Mount Pantheon. "And, like you, I also bore witness to the emperor's barbarity."

Augustine stood and channeled her darkest hate, engulfing her fists in flames. She used both fists to fire continuous flames at Kronos. He held out his hands, creating a circular wall of ice. Her hands became numb, and her insides burned. The ice was unmoved by her attempt to melt it. She dropped to her knees.

"If you're too weak to defeat even me, how do you ever expect to kill your father?"

Blood Orgy

Planet Aphrodisia—899 CD

"You're losing strength. Eat." Kronos brought a spoon filled with steaming meat up to his lips. The stew consisted of homosaur flesh and liver. He blew on it but stopped short of consuming it.

"Is the dish not to your liking?" asked the female negroid head slave standing against the wall.

Augustine ignored the twentysomething-year-old and stared at Kronos.

He finally put the food in his mouth and let the spoon clank inside the empty bowl. A young blonde retrieved the bowl and replaced it with a saucer of blueberry turnover. She refilled his wineglass. The negro left the small dining room.

"I will *not* be your fucking puppet. It is I who is ordained."

"It's a shame how one can fall so far from the tree." He addressed the legionnaires standing behind his chair. "Bring her to me." A soldier entered the kitchen and returned with his hand around the back of the slave's neck. Kronos cleared the saucer with a fist, and the legionnaire bashed the woman's head against the table in front of him and held her down. "This squirming pile of rotting flesh is one of an untold number that will be forgotten the moment it stops breathing. It's spent an entire existence in the servitude of me simply because it lacks the ability to resist. Like her ilk, she is a breathing failure who has no true purpose in this universe other than to reproduce others like it, to be ruled by gods. Look into her eyes. See the fear. I want you to taste it. The same fear Christ had realizing that his word and brothers would one day burn in Nero's garden. Do you believe Rome conquered the earth by bending to another's will? By showing *mercy*?"

Kronos held out a hand, and the second legionnaire put a blade in his palm. The slave was brought up, and Kronos gave her the weapon without looking at her. "Prove your allegiance to the throne."

"Leave her!" said Augustine.

A set of strong hands forced her back into her seat.

"Yes, My Lord." The slave ran the blade across her own throat and fell dead.

He rose from his seat. "She knew who you would become. Trillions await Rome's rule, My Empress." They escorted him to his sleeping quarters.

A legionnaire came into the kitchen and placed an object covered in a black cloth under her nose. He uncovered the silk and then joined the others. A large silver sword with its black grip shone before her. The silver seamlessly gave way to black at the sharp tip. Augustine closed her eyes and took a deep breath.

Closer to midnight, she wallowed naked on her back in a lake near the waterfall, miles away from Kronos's tribulation, though she knew that somewhere on the rocks were a couple of soldiers discreetly dispatched for her safety.

She slowly sealed her eyes and submerged under the cold water and then opened them to pry into the souls of billions of stars. An astral body blazed in the sparkling darkness between Aphrodisia's triplet moons. More followed.

Augustine felt it. The fear that had squeezed the slave's heart before she so willingly offered her life. However weak willed she'd become, she had maintained the strength to foolishly immortalize herself in the book of the dead. No fight, just submission. She tasted it, and it tasted good. The power of his unhallowed words streamed through her, enlivening her flesh.

She never admitted it openly, but she had been infatuated with Kronos since she was a teen. At Meegan's slumber parties, she would wake up and steal a piece of his dirty clothing out the hamper and masturbate herself while sniffing them. One time, she found the master-bedroom door cracked and fondled her pussy, watching him make love to a blond peasant girl. Her inner rage consumed her teenage mind and led her to poison the woman's wine as they fucked. Augustine treasured the moment she saw the woman gag and vomit her insides on the bathroom floor. One summer night, she snuck into his room, while he lay asleep naked, and took pictures of his cock for her scrapbook.

Augustine drifted to the top. Her sensitive nipples and bosoms poked above the water like tiny islands. She panted and moaned, recalling the slave's rightful butchering.

Let them see, let them hear.

She slid a hand down her stomach and violently fingered her clit. She was desperate for more. More bodies, more blood, more power. She must have it—all of it! She caressed her hot breast with one hand and pumped her finger in and out. The lecherous young cunt couldn't control her frantic urges, her nefarious fantasies. She imagined seas of people kneeling before her galactic throne. Thousands of interstellar ships ravaging planets and enslaving its primitive natives. She was a child born in the womb of man and by the sword elevated to godhood.

Fingers tickled her shoulders, and a chest touched the top of her head.

"Lead us, My Empress," he said softly. His fingers moved to her nipples and lightly squeezed them.

"Ugh."

His hands slithered to her waist and gently pushed down to bring her chest and shoulders above the water. Her toes snuggled into the soft sand. She reached behind her neck to touch his pristine mane. His abs and erection patted her tush. His lips and tongue kissed and licked her wet neck.

Augustine began to spread her feet apart in the sand. Without hesitation, she extended her hand around her waist to clasp a hardened cock. Her teenage fantasies had taken physical form. Her womanly fingers were forbidden from closing, and they traveled forever along its veiny road. He kissed her shoulder as she tucked his manhood into her pussy.

Kronos seized the emperor's daughter's hips and backed her ass up over and over again. A god she was, but in the flesh and in her heart, she remained a carnivorous whore. A nymph who'd shackle thousands for her personal orgy. She'd slay their wives, mothers, and daughters only to use the blood as a lubricant to masturbate their surviving husbands, sons, and brothers.

"Fuck me, dammit!" she demanded. "Fuck. Ugh!"

"I am at your will, My Empress."

Her veins boiled, and Kronos continued to grow inside her.

"Do it! Do it!"

"Aggh!"

Augustine's hole sucked down the deep volcanic eruption that oozed between her thighs. Kronos smacked and pumped his hairy crotch against the girl's young ass cheeks. He slowed in pace, and she oohed and aghed at the cock that evenly slipped back and forth.

Sweat and lake water soaked her piping skin. He pulled out, and she turned to face him. She'd never seen anyone so beautiful and strong. A portion of his to-die-for hair was beneath the water. The universe reflected in his deep-blue eyes. His skin appeared to have been washed in a fountain of youth. Augustine placed her arms atop his shoulders, closed her eyes, and locked lips. Lost in lust, she detected him breaking away from her. She was left standing in the dark water, watching his chiseled back return to the shore.

The Light of God

Inferno, Planet
Athena—Hephaestus 35, 899 CD

The two legionnaires passed through a dark residential district between old houses. Garages were empty, and front doors were left open. The owners must've tried their luck outside the city limits—the least-populated areas. There was nothing else for them here. The alien attack and Omega had killed the syncorium servers. The people were now nomads doing their best to survive. Codex retained a small amount of hope that his wife and son had found a safe commune. Even if they had, the emperor was not off the hook.

This area was where Inferno's privileged citizens resided, which only meant he was close to Jupiter's Temple. Crop failure was so prevalent in Inferno that the people begged Sentinel to construct a templum honoring the god, who'd breathe life into the soil. The state-approved pontifex maxi-mus, Sexus Pontius Epidius, led the blind in a daily ritual for rains that never came. Desperate men offered coin, their virgin sons, and themselves for their families, at his urg-ing. Only he could carry the people's prayers to the god and deliver *His* message.

Bryana raised her rifle at a man who'd stirred in his sleep on a doorstep. He slept on his back, with half his body slumped on the staircase. A liquor bottle sat upright at the bottom of the steps, and miscellaneous coins lay about. Poor bastard was probably homeless and had gotten drunk in celebration of striking a gold mine.

"An invasion on the verge of wiping out humankind, and we're the only ones dumb enough to try to stop it." Bryana humphed through the secure microphone. "Now that Sentinel's reared its ugly ass, do you have any regrets?"

His only regret was the horrible fight that had caused him to drive twenty miles to his favorite pissing hole. Or the extra time he had spent processing logistics orders, after duty hours, that had caused him to miss his son's first wrestling match and the ones after. Or the time he—

It was a mistake, he often told himself. A goddamn mis-take. But Patricia's bruised eye and cracked ribs, as she held his unborn child, said otherwise. Young, dumb, and drunk. Had he thanked his father for showing him how to raise a family, or his black-and-blue mother, who had taught him the meaning of forgiveness?

"I'll assume that'll be a no. You're a hard charger. Soldier to the end, no matter what," Bryana said sarcastically. "A real go-getter—"

"You made your point, Sergeant."

He heard an automatic burst and a woman scream.

"How do they live like this?" asked Bryana. "You'd think an extraterrestrial intelligence threatening our home would pull us together. But I digress. What do they want with this guy, anyway? Wouldn't it make more sense for Sentinel to send a legion, if he was that important?"

"And shoot hungry civilians in the process? The operation would be a media fiasco. Humankind at war with the Dr'og and themselves. She was right. The people are not the enemy. And as far as I'm concerned, the aliens are just looking for a new home. Colonizers."

"Phoenix lead," transmitted the pilot.

"Shoot it."

"You got blockades, patrols, unmanned weaponry around the temple. It's gonna be hell getting to Shogun. I'll scan overhead for a way in."

"Why do I get the feeling we're being followed?" said Bryana.

Codex had been feeling it too, since hitting the high-end neighborhood. He switched the visor's internal image to the rear camera and then back. He scanned for movement in the houses to his left and right. A passing wind circulated sand and creaked doors.

"Dr'og?" asked Bryana.

When Codex's eyes centered back on the road, a figure in a hooded white toga was frozen in their path. A scarf covered his mouth and nose. "Someone else." The sergeant drew her rifle. The master legionnaire's visor read that the figure was twenty-nine feet away.

"Is that who I think it is?"

"The pontifex maximus."

The priest spread his hands. "Lay down your weapons, my children. This is the beginning."

"What the fuck he is on?" said Bryana.

"You need to move fast, or you're gonna be fighting your way out of an ambush," transmitted the pilot.

Codex knew the pontifex would never leave the temple unguarded. The figure became embedded in a brewing sandstorm, and his neck stretched toward the sky.

A detonation resonated through Codex's armor and off abandoned houses and nearby vehicles. The sandstorm partially blinded his view of a descending fireball. A weapon fired to Codex's right. He switched to night vision and saw the priest's shoulder jar back. Amber bullets homed in his direction from eleven and one. Codex split left and slid, with one leg under the other. He braced on the rear of a parked rover and engaged a group of men who were deploying into the street.

"Stop!" demanded the pontifex. His words breached Codex's secure net. The last bullet pinged off the road. "I know you can hear me. But you do not understand. Understand the things I've seen, learned, felt."

Codex's heads-up display went black.

"The darkness, my savior's eternal enemy. I begged to see the light! Yet he hid it from me for years. I clawed at his skin and searched for it. It never came. He forced me to feed off the scarce vermin that dined on the insects in his depths. Broke my avaricious soul and showed me the true...meaning of life. Not survival, not material wealth, not endless feasts, or lust!"

Communicating with Bryana was not an option. He needed to find a way to get her attention.

The priest's voice became louder. "And when my filthy and sinful flesh was hanging from the skin of my dry bones and my will was no more...he came to me. Shining brighter than ever before. He spoke unto my being: 'Deliver My message to the people of Athena and to those of Earth. Deliver it throughout the galaxy. But do not fear the savages of the nether regions. Correct their ways and unite them under my words. For you have seen hell, and those who deny My tongue will see this as well.'"

Codex removed his helmet, keeping his earpiece in place and his eyes closed. He felt around the helmet's back for a hidden panel. He popped it open to retrieve a set of black digital glasses. He put them on and set the thermal imager. The priest remained standing where he had last seen him. Codex completed a rough scan of the area for his missing partner.

"I returned to Athena and followed God's commandment to sacrifice my beloved wife as an offering for His forgiveness. I stabbed her and her adulterer as they lay together in sin. I, a descendant of Moses, carried God's word to the poor, and they mocked me. 'Heresy!' they cried. But when the demons fell from grace and the people's false prophet fled in the face of Satan, they sought out His word, just as I had."

Codex sneaked to the driver's-side door and aimed his weapon at the location he'd last seen his target. The rifle moved counterclockwise. He pressed the galea crest on his muscle cuirass's upper right breast and sidestepped left out of cover. The cloak was an internal feature, preventing Matt's stolen technology from commandeering it. Codex inhaled through his nostrils to his minimize the chances of swallowing swirling sand. The winds pounded at his earpiece, and Matt was nowhere to be found.

The master legionnaire returned to the center of the street and moved forward with his weapon steadied ahead. A heavy object whirled around his weapon. The rifle's grip was wrenched from his hands.

Crack! A fist pummeled his eye. A kick to his center abdomen. A chain-like sound dragged against the ground. Metal sank into his armor, traveling across a shoulder and down his spine.

"Urrgh!"

"Yeah, motherfucker. I told y'all niggas to beat feet." The chain scraped against the pavement. "Seem like someone didn't get da message."

Wfff! Clank! "Aggh!"

"Enough!" cried Matt.

"Roll yo ass ova." Shogun jammed his boot under Codex's chest and tipped him faceup. "Gimme dat."

Robbed of his digital glasses, the master legionnaire barely made out the hooded toga and hanging dreadlocks. An amber light pulsated above Shogun's shoulder.

"Bring him, while there's still a soul left to be saved."

VISIONS

PLANET UNKNOWN, DATE UNKNOWN

The star's morning rays soaked into Augustine's skin, leaving a smile on her face. She lay in the soft grass, watching passing clouds. A flock of four drakons easily separated their whiteness with their thick wings. Her nostrils inhaled air so pellucid that it was inconceivable that humankind had ever existed.

How long had she been here? How did she get here? It didn't matter. What did was that she was finally at peace. Augustine sat up on the tush of her high blue-jean shorts, leaving her fingers in the grass.

The teen's skin chilled and prickled. She heard and felt every beat of her heart. She began to move upright. Her knees felt too weak to withstand this world's beauty. Her mouth partially opened.

Unimaginable architecture that transcended man's capabilities had been erected in a mountain valley. Glass-like skyscrapers touched the heavens. She didn't know what to make of the floating energy fields that supported what seemed like small domiciles. Several aerial transports that were long in design shot from pillar to post before she could bat an eyelid. Augustine held a salute above her eyebrow and squinted at the water flowing out of the mountain. She saw no beginning or lake at its end; it magically flowed and disappeared into nowhere.

In a blazing instant, she was conveyed to a bustling street. Gray beings who wore woolen clothes went about their business, entering and exiting shops. Pushing newborns in strollers that hovered. Dishing out slabs of hot meat, without the exchange of funds. Augustine sensed an unconditional love among the aliens, though they spoke no words or had mouth parts to do so. Flying rovers—her only word to describe them—zigged above her head. Tens walked by her yet seemed not to notice her presence.

A lone alien paused by Augustine's side. A holographic frame appeared in front of his face. This one had a semblance of woe about him, and she sensed every bit of it. He reached a hand to the hologram and typed a series of hieroglyphics. He lowered his gray head, and the hologram faded.

To her amazement, he rotated his body in her direction. His head cocked sideways like a mystified dog. Augustine's nerves brimmed with bewilderment.

He sees me.

The extraterrestrial lifted one of two fingers and tapped the center of her forehead. His appearance began to melt, and her mind became flooded with horror. Everything melted as she grabbed both sides of her head. The sky revamped into a deep and starless black. Lightning cracked above. The once-tranquil aliens were now levitating around her. Their hands glowed a deep red, and their avaricious souls radiated conceit. They gave no diligence for their fellow beings.

Again, the scenery changed. However, this time she sailed midair above a large and glowing red dome made of glass. The terrain held a very familiar appearance. But the cliffs to the northwest, northeast, southeast, and southwest were mega ramps. The ramps curved down from the top to the dome's base.

Inside the glass was a dark-red orb. She saw aliens hovering on a small staircase into the structure. The dome started to spin at indescribable speeds. Augustine was soon trapped in a red funnel that shot far above the planet and into outer space.

She screamed and covered her ears, and then her world went black. Space and time ceased to exist. Suddenly she was an observer, in outer space, to a gigantic relay system for the orb's light. She could see Athena below. The system was circular and allowed the red funnel to pass through its center. But nothing came out on the other side.

It was happening again. Her body zipped through the system and rapidly appeared above an unfamiliar green-and-blue planet. Without a moment's notice, she was channeled down to the planet's surface.

The land was much different from the one she had left. She discerned an overall feeling of primitivism. Augustine saw stone buildings, houses, and village fires spread throughout the green hills and pastures. A large cloud loomed over a snow-covered mountain. Despite the primordial ways of whoever inhabited this world, she also detected their wisdom.

Her first remote encounter with the natives was seeing a four-legged and four-armed green alien haul wood on his shoulders from a stone house to a fire pit. The muscular beast had an air of patriotism and honor for his land and people. Two little ones scampered behind him. Their hearts were made of respect and followership.

And soon, the sky ripped opened just as it had at the palace that fateful morning. Miles and miles away, the orb's red light dropped behind the mountain. The children's caregiver hurried them back into the house. He himself returned outside with the same weapon his kind had used to kill her people. More armed Dr'og exited their homes. Patches of land lifted to reveal hovering one-seater cycles. They jumped on their vehicles and went off toward the light.

As before, the scene melted away, and moss now covered the stone houses. High grass hid the fire pits. The sky was a bottomless black, with shots of lightning.

Augustine willingly closed her eyes and waited. When she reopened them, the Dr'og were in a ferocious firefight with the Ereb, who used elemental magic as weapons. Pain, so much pain, but she could not deny her joy in seeing the weak slaughtered. Their stone cities burned and crumbled. Statues of their four-armed leaders toppled. Millions of natives were killed. The survivors were taken as slaves and forced onto diamond-shaped spaceships. They deserved the brutality lashed upon their race. The galactic battlefield was no playground. Every species for itself. The Ereb's evolutionary superiority was undeniable, but their bodies and minds were weak—a stark contrast to the Roman Empire, her empire. Just when she had seen enough, an eruption occurred to her south. The red light had died.

As Augustine turned back around, a Dr'og aimed a weapon at her face and pulled the trigger.

▲   ▲   ▲

PLANET APHRODISIA—899 CD

Augustine jumped up in bed, staring into a dawn-lit room. Wind blasted through an open wooden window that creaked. An orange Helios ascended behind the mountains. She got from under the covers and stood, putting a hand to her sweaty head. Seeing that she was only wearing a white T-shirt, she quickly picked up a black-and-gray plaid sweater off a wooden chair. After slipping into a pair of ankle-length blue-jean shorts, she left the bedroom.

She fast paced it down a small series of steps that led to the front door. She stopped, never touching the handle.

His fingers slowly tapped the wooden kitchen table.

"Why are you doing this?" Augustine asked, facing the door.

No response.

"I don't want to see any more. Do you hear me? No more!"

A final tap.

"You have the strength of a thousand Roman soldiers and the philosophy of an imbecile."

Augustine used a hand to pry the unlocked door open, and the wind did the rest. She heard the kitchen chair scoot against the floor.

Her dark hair and clothes flapped as she walked away from the cabin, and she only stopped when he spoke.

His raised voice was mixed into the turbulent morning winds. "The GodSphere's power only extended so far. After the Ereb discovered the primitive Dr'og's home world, they enslaved as many as they could to dig for the planet's sphere. But their powers waned over the vast distance from Athena. Their attempts to chain the sphere's power throughout the solar system was a disaster. The Dr'og turned the tide, and the Ereb had no choice but to replicate the sphere. Their infantile logic of the universe caused a fatal reaction. The detonation on Athena destroyed the planet's topside. Their leaders planned for this, which is why they bred a subterranean civilization."

Augustine didn't face Kronos. Instead, she continued to watch the rising sun.

"You cannot destroy life. It will continue to exist if the universe wills it to. Some spheres take trillions of years to produce life, but evolution will go on."

Augustine hesitated but soon turned to meet a bare-chested Kronos. "They didn't come for us or the sphere. They came for them, and we're in the way."

"The Dr'og are an unforgiving race. Intelligent, peaceful—but do not cross them. Once they defeated the remaining Ereb, they reverse engineered their technology and brought the war to them."

"And the Dr'og believe we're helping the Ereb."

Kronos didn't say anything after that.

"You…you're helping them. It's not the empire you want me to lead. It's them."

"Man, in his current state, is a doomed species. Emperor Cenaeus learned this when the probes that launched in AD 2287 returned their findings on Athena."

"Rome knew about what happened on Athena. Why go?"

"Domination. What better display of Roman power than to conquer an alien world? The last three emperors of the Cenaeus bloodline made first contact with the Ereb. They drank the alien blood in exchange for the deliverance of a GodSphere to resurrect their fallen society. We will be greatly rewarded."

Augustine said, "The human body doesn't have to harness the sphere's raw energy to amass its power."

"Precisely."

"How did the sphere remain hidden for so long?"

"The ultimate form of power. Dark energy."

Augustine felt cold.

"Energy never mastered by the Ereb. They, like several other worlds, discovered the sphere by chance. You are the epitome of our evolution. Your heart is as dark as your mother's. I spoke with the elders and was granted my right to regicide. And it is also my right to use the sword of another."

Augustine started to walk away.

"Face me!" yelled Kronos. "I'm tired of playing games with you, child."

She balled her fists.

"I saved you from your father, showed you your true self, and fulfilled your deviant fantasies. And you spit in my face. Your mother turns in her grave at the thought of you. Your worthless empire is nothing but that. I offer you real supremacy. The throne of the universe. I see the only thing you're good for is what's between your legs. Teenage whore—you certainly are your father's child."

Augustine's eyes turned hot, and her fists roasted. She swung around and extended her flamed fists at Kronos, knocking him into the air and past the cabin. With her sweater unbuttoned, she advanced at him, turning her fiery fists into ice. Kronos shuddered, trying to stand. She jumped up and drove a cold set of knuckles into his chest, dispersing the shards.

Augustine saw legionnaires in her peripheral run out of the cabin. One tossed a Serpent Blade at Kronos, who was starting to stand. He caught the blade and came erect. Each man transformed into an ice pillar. Augustine twisted her hands, crunched her fists, and shattered them. The sound of their crunched bones and screams was a mental orgasm.

"Learn to control your—"

Augustine used both hands to lift Kronos off his feet. His demand was more like a plea—a plea for mercy that she did not have.

Kronos choked and placed his hands around his neck. His legs kicked. The vision of his useless struggle and restricted breaths doused her skin in a lustful sweat.

"You think you can rule the empire hiding behind my back?"

Kronos fell, and his leg crunched. "Aggh!"

She came to stand over him. "You need me, sniveling bitch. Let this be a lesson. Do not bite the hand that feeds," snarled Kronos.

Augustine's hair blew across her face in the relentless winds. As she stared down at Kronos, her body temperature raised.

"Your eyes. Don't do this. You're not ready."

She spread her arms to the side and saw irregular black circles form out of thin air. She exhaled as the darkness spread into her blood. She opened her palms at Kronos. A black sickness traveled up his white skin and through his veins. He cried out.

"The empire belongs to me" were her final words to him as his skin melted into a black goo. The sun rose behind her back. His face, a hand, and strands of white hair were the only body parts discernible in the thick sludge.

BEND OVER AND TAKE IT

TARTARUS, TEMPLE OF JUPITER, INFERNO, PLANET ATHENA—DATE UNKNOWN

They had stripped him of his weapons and armor. Bound and blindfolded him. Next thing he knew, he was tossed in a steel cage somewhere inside the temple's humid depths.

Codex sat on a dusty mat with his forearms crossed atop his knees. His tired eyes had grown accustomed to the dark, and when his cheeks brushed his skin, he felt overgrowth. His black undershirt was tied across his stinging bicep.

He heard the wooden plate that contained leftover scraps move. Tiny claws skedaddled on the floor, and the metal bars rang.

Codex turned his eyes to the cage, hearing the creature squeal under a boot. He returned to the wall in front of him.

"I could have you killed; do you know this?" asked Matt.

Codex spat bread seeds that'd he loosened from his molars.

"But I am a messenger of peace. The new rock from which His church will be built."

He spat out more seeds.

"Even *she* came to me in her time of need. My heart could never turn away a child of God. Her clothes were on their final thread. Ignorant of God's word, she fell to her knees and begged for his forgiveness. And when I laid my hands upon her negro skin, I tasted her defilement. I took her in and consoled her on my thigh, where she confessed her sins. My generosity extended to her uncivilized chimp, at her request."

Codex blacked out and in half a second reached through the bars and grabbed Matt's cloak. The priest's face struck the cage.

"I seem to have gotten your attention."

"I'm gonna gut the fuck outta you," snarled Codex.

Matt bent over, holding his stomach. The master legionnaire seized the back of the priest's neck, keeping him arched at the waist. A door opened, and men entered the dungeon to pry the pontifex maximus from Codex's hands.

"Ready fo' round two, nigga?" said Shogun. "Open dis bitch!" His men unlocked the cage and began kicking and punching at Codex.

One of Shogun's men locked Codex into a full nelson.

Matt took down his hood. His brown hair was long, and he sported a matching goatee. "Your family is a lost cause to you, but I will kill them. And unless you do what I say, your wife and child will be raped at God's altar while you're still alive to witness it."

"Yo! Dat bitch is *yo* wife? Christ O' might, she got an ass on her. What a fine light-skinned sista doing with a white-trash nigga like you?" asked Shogun.

"You will help me and these men secure an interstellar transport. Functional cryo chambers, rations, weapons, and prepped for one of the thousands of uncivilized planets your warlords have discovered. No less. Once my demands have been met, they are yours."

"Fool, is you crazy? I'm tapping dat bitch before she go anywhere. You can keep that little man of hers. I ain't down with dis religious shit."

Codex spit in Matt's face.

"As expected. Gentlemen, it seems we have a nonbeliever on our hands."

"Night, night, muthafucka." *Punch!*

▲ ▲ ▲

COURTYARD, TEMPLE OF JUPITER, INFERNO, PLANET ATHENA—HEPHAESTUS 37, 899 CD

Whip!

"Urgh," grunted the sergeant.

Whhhack! Bryana vomited as the fifth whip cracked her bare skin. With her head and arms locked in the pillory, she kept her face cast down from the crowd but felt the condemnation of their twisted thoughts.

Her teeth gnashed into the cloth at the sixth, seventh, eighth, and then she screamed. Nine! Ten! She heard Shogun drop the whip on the wooden platform. She detected his heavy boot steps, and his pant legs contacted her rear thighs.

Bryana wiggled and squeezed her fists. His unlubed member seesawed between her ass cheeks.

"I'm the first, but I won't be the last," said Shogun.

"Rrrgh, rrrgh, eegghgh!"

The pontifex maximus had ordered a legal cleansing—a public lashing followed by a free-for-all gang rape, the ultimate form of humiliation.

Shogun extracted his cock and shoveled it into her cunt.

Bryana nearly died, sensing her salty sweat mixing into her lacerations. Shogun's hips packed his oversize piston as deep into her as her physiology would allow. He tapped her wet and sore ass twice and then went back to mauling her pussy. The molested legionnaire's willpower was trounced. She ended her inutile struggle and closed her eyes.

Shogun's valve opened and flooded her inner walls. He wasted no time sitting inside her. He slid out and zipped up. Matt's appointed strongarm came around to the pillory's front.

"Open up, bitch. You got customers." He untied the cloth and wrapped it around his knuckles.

"Do all the women you fuck need a real man to finish the job?"

Punch! Punch! Punch!

"Big man, aren't you? Beating up on defenseless girls." She hawked and spit. "Guess you gotta compensate somewhere for that inadequate cock of yours. For your sake, you better hope they don't untie me."

Punch!

He crouched next to her and whispered, "I oughta cut yo throat, talking all dat shit. Now, this can go down one of two ways. I line every one of dem niggas up and let them drown you in nut. Or...I call a few, play the game, and I come holla at you?"

"Why should I trust you?"

"Because I'm the one dats gonna keep yo ass alive. Learn to make new friends. You'll need them. Remember, the clock's ticking."

The Dark Empress

Temple of Jupiter, Inferno, Planet Athena—Hephaestus 38, 899 CD

"Move it!" demanded the slave master. Bryana watched his whip snap across a man's lower back. The tall male barked, "This doesn't involve you. Get back to work!" He spared her the rod.

She heaved, helping to pass a stone block to the girl standing next to her. The pontifex maximus wanted the temple reconstructed. The alien invasion had ruined the pillars, as well as the steps and much of the roof. She had heard a rumor that he planned to rename it the New Church of Jehovah. Athena would be the bedrock from which this religion was born. Sentinel did not forbid any religion but strongly influenced worship of the ancient Roman gods.

"Isn't he a dreamboat?" asked the girl next to her. Her brunette hair was tied into a ponytail. Like the others, she wore the obligatory brown tunic and sandals. Her white skin was stained with dirt and smelled of pickles.

The slave master blew the whistle.

"Yeah?" Bryana was afforded a break. She bent over, picked up a leather water pouch, and guzzled. The water nearly scalded her tongue.

"Not the pontifex, if that's who you think I meant. *Him*." Her tone was awfully chirpy for a *slave*. That went for all the reborn, a name Matt's baptized followers took on. Only the reborn were exempt from slave-like labor. The reborn performed medical procedures and governmental tasks, gave legal advice, and taught the Book of Graesen to all. Matt showed favoritism toward professionals and quickly baptized them. And, judging by what she'd seen, very few had been reborn.

"The slave master?"

"Watch your tongue with who you say that around," replied the girl. "I know I'm still considered a born until our leader baptizes me. But I can't resist when Octavianus corrects me with that long whip he got there. Sometimes I even mess up just to feel it. I saw you the other day sexing that nigger. I wish that was me up there. All tied up, defenseless, and with a sweaty negro cock between my legs." She shivered.

"You're a fucking nut."

The girl laughed. "I know. Isn't this place wonderful?"

"Why do you do it?"

"I just get so damn"—she leaned to whisper—"horny."

"I'm talking about following this make-believe shit."

The girl frowned. "Unlike you, I can think on my own. I got annoyed with my father and his wife and their bottomless bag of coin. The attack was my ticket to redemption. Whatever happened to them ain't none of mine. The pontifex and this commune is everything I've ever needed. He preaches the truth, and"—she leaned in again—"don't tell, but I've seen it myself."

I'm sure every woman in this place will soon enough. Bryana internalized her antagonizing thoughts.

"One night, I was scrubbing the communications-room floor, and when I left, I saw this green light at the end of the corridor." Octavianus blew the whistle. "And Shogun's boys were guarding it. They said to me, 'Bitch, you better move along, or you gonnas gets the D.' 'The D' means dick. I learned that from one of the other girls. I should have stayed put. Ha! I ain'ts allowed down there no more."

"Yeah, I know what it means. So there's a comm room?"

"Some people don't believe the Light is real. If you haven't heard him preach, you should. God must have really trusted the pontifex to lead his people. Showing him the way and all from the Light. It's something *real* special to be the only person who can see God's words. But he preaches that jealousy is a sin, and we should all accept our place in this world. Some are just more holier-than-thou, and it's their responsibility to lead us to God and his son, Jesus."

"Hey, let's go," said a male born.

Bryana took the stone and handed it off to the girl.

"Do you remember where it's at?"

The girl kept quiet and cupped her arms to take the next stone.

"So now you're deaf?"

"Shut the fuck up over there!" protested a born. "Before we all get a lash." The whip cracked some bodies down from Bryana.

The girl said, "I know what you're trying to do. You ain'ts leaving this place. He'll make a believer out of you, if it's the last thing he does."

After the day's work ended, a freshly rinsed Bryana sat at a large communal feasting table for the born. Sustenance was given twice a day to all followers. Matt's belief was that full workers labored at their best. Since her release from the Tartarus, she ate seasoned pancakes and drank two glasses of water for ientaculum. Cena varied, from toasted turkey sandwiches to porridge. She twisted her head to see the reborn at their table, feasting on roasted pig and Dr'og meat that made the entire room smell like fish guts. The pontifex maximus and Shogun's men ate alone at another location in the templum.

Bryana smelled shampoo and heard someone plop next to her.

"Hi," said whatever her name. The girl's hair was wet and stranded over her face. "Pompeia, since you never asked me."

"Bryana," said the sergeant. She crunched her fried hog's fat sandwich.

"I think I know why you got cleansed."

She washed down loose bread particles. At least someone did. All she remembered was being pulled out of the Tartarus and lashed in the courtyard.

"You see, you're not as strong as your partner. The pontifex preaches that no woman is stronger than a man. You're less of an escape risk if you know what could happen."

"The room. Where is it?" whispered Bryana.

Pompeia cut her sandwich into two halves. She said, "That pig looks delicious. I can't wait to be reborn." Pompeia's elbow bumped her water cup, spilling it onto the floor. "Whoops." She put two fingers to her lips. "I'm such a loser." She created an *L* with her thumb and index finger and sat it on her forehead. She used a napkin to wipe the water and then refilled the cup from a wooden pitcher.

"Stop fucking around. I can get us both out of here."

"Listen—but you didn't hear this from me." Pompeia moved closer. "I heard that he's taking us out of this darn, awful place. Some other world where the people ain'ts never heards of God or Jesus. Ain't that silly?" She put two fists on her hips. "Well, he's gonna have to show them a thing or two."

Octavianus rang the sustenance bell. "Let's go! Prayer and slumber. You got a lot of work ahead of you come daybreak."

"Whelp, that's my cue. Bedtime."

"Number Twenty-Seven!" called out Octavianus, whose chest was protected by a muscle cuirass. "New room assignment." He came over as Bryana stood up. "Twenty-four-B. There was a sewage accident above your old room. Not going into details. Now get the hell out of my sight."

Bryana did her best not to snatch the fork off the table and jab it into his fucking Adam's apple.

"Same thing, Number Twelve. Shit leaked down to the first floor. New room, same as hers."

"Oh, my goody! We're roommates."

Bryana looked around the room at the departing diners for Shogun but didn't locate him.

Five minutes after she and Pompeia entered the new room, someone had locked it from the outside. It resembled her previous one: white walls, two beds covered with gray blankets, a nightstand, the Book of Graesen, clothes dresser, and a small restroom with a toilet and sink. Bryana was sitting on the side of her stiff bed when Pompeia got under her covers and opened her Bible. The little bitch's cheeks gleefully shone, being brainwashed into peonage.

On the dot, the lights went out, and the air conditioner kicked on. Bryana's eyes had a moment before they were able to adjust to the darkness. She heard a thud, and Pompeia moved in her bed.

"You frontliners really need to learn the art of patience. Do you really think anyone in their right mind would believe this shit? I can't fathom you swallowed that story out there. A soldier like you wouldn't last one hour on the first day."

"Black Legion."

"Two years and counting."

"We were sent in to capture the pontifex and bring him back alive."

"Let's be honest here. No, you weren't. Sentinel used you as bait for something much darker. My job was to make sure you called in the cavalry for backup, once you located the target, and didn't commit sedition against the empire."

"How did you get captured?"

"That little hair that stood on the back of your head was me. Codex's intuition about Matt was right. He's the pontifex, and the empire is unaware of this. I didn't suspect he was able to hack our communications. I buried my gear and stripped down. To them, I'm a lost soul needing redemption."

"You risked your life to save us?"

"Happy to see me?"

"The communications room."

Pompeia put two fingers to her lips and then made an L with her fingers on her forehead. "West of the templum, second level. Never seen it but know someone who did."

Water. She remembered the spilled cup and the girl saying "Whoops."

"What about Shogun?"

"He has his own agenda. Advanced weapons, vehicles, money. He was onto me from the moment I turned my oh-so-needy soul over. He wasn't buying it. He's a lifelong criminal who's been in Sentinel's crosshairs since he came out of the womb."

"The accident was no accident at all."

Knock, knock. The door unlatched, and Bryana's vision had adjusted well enough to see two negro men enter. One closed it behind him. "Boss said y'all too lonely and need some company."

"Who's lonely when they's gots Jesus?"

"Shut the fuck up, bitch. I'll take this one. Turn dat ass over."

Pompeia got on all fours on the bed. *Kick!* He held his throat and struggled for air.

"Yo! What the—"

Bryana snagged the second man's head as he attempted to assail the undercover operative. His neck cracked left to right.

Pompeia's victim fell over on his side, losing the fight. It wasn't long before he gave up. Shogun had given them the pink slip to take their cut.

"We need to send a signal to the nearest outpost and wait for extraction," Pompeia said.

"Codex—we can't leave him."

"I don't intend to."

"Shit. They're unarmed," said Bryana, patting down the dead men.

"You'll figure it out. He said he'd keep things light until we reached the communications room."

The sergeant opened the door and peeked into the stone corridor. Torches lit a long path to the left. Along the corridor were separate rooms that housed the other borns. The two women hightailed it to the corridor's entrance. The sounds of their sandals slapped against the layered walls. Pompeia tied up her long hair into a ponytail as they reached the end.

Bryana cracked the wooden Roman arched door and observed reborns, with their backs to her, sitting in a semi-circle around a fire. One of them stood near the flames. His lips moved as he looked down at what she assumed was the

Bible. She took the first chance to dash into the open when the preacher turned around. Pompeia tagged behind her to a horse and carriage.

"That's it over there," said the operative, pointing at a one-level stone structure to the temple's west. Lucky for them, multiple opportunities for concealment were along the route.

"The Book of Graesen tells us that God's messenger rose from the dead. Reborn in the image of our Lord and Savior, Jesus Christ!" sermonized the teacher. "Chosen to deliver the light into all of our dark and sinful souls. Rejoice, children! For the time of salvation is upon us."

Bryana continued to crouch and repositioned herself behind an unoccupied fruit-and-bread stand. When Octavianus was feeling generous, he'd allow his workers to snack from the stands. Pompeia came close, stole a green apple, and bit in.

The preacher continued. "How many of you here are struggling to let go of your sinful ways? All of us are. Even me. But we must remember that God wants us to struggle. It is his will. Do not succumb to the ways of the unsaved lowbrow and give in to temptation. I see that we have a few negros joining us tonight. Understand that God made you three-eighths of a human for a reason. As saved lowbrows, you must reach out to your fellow dark skins and show them how God has helped you. You have the greatest struggle of us all. However, in the Kingdom of Heaven, your struggles will not go unrewarded. So the chosen has written."

"Amen."

Bryana shook her head and sighed. "Are they all like this?" she asked Pompeia, coming to a quiet horse stable.

"They came here seeking whatever the Dr'og took from them: shelter, food, a warm bed, religion. They'll believe in anything to have the semblance of a normal life again."

The aliens had killed Bryana's elderly mother and father. Their apartment in downtown Utopis had crumbled under the impact of missiles. She was their only child and was all they had. Codex and Sentinel had separate interests, and she had hers. Her fight was with the invaders who had taken the only thing she cared about. She had declared her own personal war and promised to hunt and kill every Dr'og left on the planet.

Bryana and Pompeia stopped at the stable's far corner. A dreaded thug exited the targeted building, letting the door close on its own. He smoked a cigarette with a Dr'og rifle on his shoulder.

The man walked over to join the nighttime congregation.

A loud and repeating siren was heard. "All followers return to your quarters. This is not a drill. All followers return to your quarters. This is not a drill."

Bryana remembered what Shogun said to her: "The clock's ticking."

"Over there!" someone behind her said. The man fired amber rounds at a fleeing born. The escapee's arms went into the air, and he dropped knee first in the sand. The study group covered their mouths while the speaker ushered them to their quarters.

"Let's be quick about this," said Bryana. A few more men left the communications structure and rounded up the remaining flock. She led Pompeia to the next way point, the rear of an unoccupied blacksmith forge. Wasting not another second, she sprinted over to the building's left wall. The side ran longer than it appeared to from the forge. She abandoned the idea of entering through the front and kept against the wall to the rear.

"One," said Bryana after peeking around the edge. The man was guarding what was more than likely a ramp that led underground. She hadn't noticed it before, but two guards manned opposing watchtowers that faced the building. "A little overboard, don't you think?" she asked Pompeia. The brown-haired girl didn't respond.

Just then, a full-size truck pulled up to the tower's base and went black. Bryana saw the guards leave their post and begin climbing down the ladder.

As the man flipped around to descend the ramp, Bryana ran and hopped over the short wall. She put him in a headlock with her left bicep, unsheathed his boot knife, and plunged it into his heart. She did it again and then twelve more times till his chest became a surging fire hydrant. The knife entered his kidney and twisted. He fell, cold and lifeless. She broke off the keycard that was chained around his neck and swiped it on a pad to the ramp's left. The ground-level door retracted. They entered, and she keyed it closed.

The path was dark, save for a few long fluorescent lights evenly spaced on a slanted ceiling. Pompeia kept behind Bryana, who moved slowly down the floor with her back to the smooth wall and the weapon at her side, ready to claim another casualty. She stopped at the end, just short of expos-ing her body in a corridor. She surveyed the other side to see an armed goon patrolling the area. The ceiling was absent any lights, and she saw the orange ashes of his flicked cigarette. He stopped but started again in her direction. Bryana returned to concealment and listened to his boot steps.

A blind swing to the left. She felt the knife grind against bone and extracted the blade from his throat. Her dripping weapon and hand caught the back of his head and forced him around the corner.

Bryana and Pompeia moved into the open and went prone. They high crawled beneath the seal of an expansive glass window. *Almost there.* Her elbows alternated on the hard floor. Midway through the glass, a door opened outward. A small object slipped out of the departing occupant's rear pants pocket. He made a left into the next corridor.

Bryana sped up and swiped a second keycard, labeled CR. She and Pompeia got back on their feet once they cleared the glass.

"There should be only one room on this corridor."

"We're good," said Bryana. She moved into position and flagged the card reader to open the sliding door. They both entered, and she listened to the entrance resecure itself.

"There's no power," said Pompeia.

Bryana's pinkie toe kicked a plastic object, causing it to glare as it rolled. She bent over to pick up the object, a flashlight, and flicked it on. Shogun had colored her a yellow-brick road, but at what cost? Weapons and technology were only the beginning.

She shone the light over a cobwebbed communications console that hadn't seen use since the Defiance Wars. She knew the temple's grounds had served as an insurgent base during the infamous conflict. Bryana envisioned how brave the rebels had been for standing up against a continued monarchist government. The people claimed Rome had slowly abandoned the ancient republic after Athena had been conquered.

"This thing is two hundred years old," said Pompeia, coughing at the cloud that circulated when she dusted off a keyboard.

Bryana shone the beam against the wall, revealing a lever. "Let's hope this works."

Clunk.

Small trinkets and gizmos flickered a deep blue. Three hidden screens livened with static—as well as a microphone on the console.

"Let's go home," said Pompeia as Bryana approached the console.

Bryana jammed her knuckles on the keyboard's sides. "Understand that home and everything we've ever cared about is dead. Gone—you got that? Once the master legionnaire is out safe, I'm cutting ties with Sentinel." She typed in the global coordinates for Outpost Fury.

"Fury to transmitter. Identify your unit, shield number, and position."

"Fury, this is Sergeant Legionnaire Vitoria Bryana of Phoenix Squad. Shield, 19872. Master Legionnaire Codex and I have been taken captive and are being held at Jupiter's Temple. Requesting immediate search and rescue."

A pause.

"Copy that. Has the target been located?"

"Affirmative. Matt's the pontiff. Bring enough firepower."

"Evac in twenty mike."

A pain shot through Bryana's back. Her chest smashed onto the console. She slumped to the floor and then heard the door open. Pompeia leaned over and laughed in the injured sergeant's face. "Fooled you twice. Shame on you, missy."

The hooded pontiff and Shogun stood over her head. Matt said to Shogun, "Ready the prisoner. I only need one ship. God have mercy on those who don't make it."

"And this one?" asked his henchman.

"She served her purpose in this world. Send her to the Lord. For He who sits at the right hand of the father judges both the living"—Matt walked away—"and the dead." The door closed.

Shogun aimed the Dr'og rifle down at her. Bryana tucked one foot under her bottom and jolted herself backward. She listened to the power of her kick as he hit the lever. Bryana ran after him and performed a jump kick. He ducked, and she dropped her weight to avoid a shot from the weapon. She punched the weapon as he pulled the trigger, and she landed a left across his jaw. He fumbled to her right, and she hooked her fingers into his armor's upper rear side. She climbed on his back and used her thighs to lock his neck.

Snap!

Bryana landed on solid ground with his head between her sandals. She armed herself.

"They made me do it," said Pompeia. "I swear."

Bryana pointed the weapon at the double-crossing bitch.

Splat! The sergeant added brain matter, flesh, and skull fragments to the room's decor.

A wavering alarm sounded. Bryana left the two dead assholes in the communications room and stepped into the corridor. A red beacon circled on the ceiling at the corridor's end.

A PA came on. "This is not a drill, children. This is the day we've all been waiting for. Prepared for. Soldiers, take up your arms and fight so your brethren can leave this world and spread the light of God among the stars."

Bryana broke neck down the corridor, flipped a right, and continued up the ramp. She opened the door, looked to the dark sky above, and said, "The emperor." The ruler's distinguishable black and slanted V-Wing craft was on the approach, protected by several Devil's Wings that started firing on Shogun's crew. She watched them descend on the temple's grounds. Legionnaires deployed out of the craft and returned fire.

Bryana sprinted across the compound in the direction of the Tartarus, ducking and dodging bullets. The legionnaires slew everyone in their path, without a sliver of mercy. Borns, reborns—even children—could not escape death. In the heat of battle, she witnessed an armed group escort Matt and a wrist-bound Codex out of the one-level stone prison.

She took off a thug's head and the shit stain next to him. The pontiff pointed for them to take her out. She squeezed the Dr'og rifle's trigger, and the grip became hot. The barrel glowed amber, and sonic rounds fled the alien weapon's chambers, punching holes in chests and abdomens. Codex fell as Bryana came closer. She heard a halt in fire behind her, and the weapon's circular green lights on the barrel died. She trashed the weapon and busted ass at Matt.

Knee! Punch!

"We're getting out of here," said Bryana, untying the rope that bound Codex.

"Patricia. My son. Where are they!" demanded the master legionnaire as he massaged his wrists.

Matt wobbled to his feet and threw a picture at them. "In hell or slave to the beast that is man." He laughed as Codex, on his knees, picked up the family photograph.

"This entire place is one big mind fuck. We'll find your family," said Bryana, helping him up. She grabbed a Dr'og rifle off a dead body, ready to send this fucker to his false god and bastard son. Suddenly an unknown force pulled the weapon from her grip.

"You have something that is mine," said Thaddeus. He crushed the alien weapon in half with one hand. He listened to his soldiers aim their rifles at Matt. Flames reflected off the fugitive's face. "Give it to me."

"Aggh!" battle cried a male, lunging at the emperor.

"No!" shouted his bald comrade.

Thaddeus used a hand to shove gravity at the two. He watched their helpless bodies bash against the building behind them.

"The sphere."

The pontiff had perfected the skill of blocking his thoughts. He knew more than what he led his followers to believe. Matt dared to quote a long-forgotten scripture in the emperor's presence. "Let no man deceive you by any means; for that day shall not—"

Thaddeus saw bullets fly his way. He used his hands to create a shield of ice. He smashed his iron fist into it once he heard the weapon click.

He extended his claw and summoned the man off his feet. He trapped his neck in it.

The emperor smiled and asked, "Is that so? Master Legionnaire Darius Codex, is it? Die knowing that I sacrificed them for the good of my empire."

Thaddeus choke slammed Codex on the ground. He put a boot on his chest and extracted the mini machine gun from the gauntlet. Codex yelled to his partner, "Kill the priest! I saw the emperor's plan. Kill him!"

As soon as Matt turned his back to run, a shank went through his skull.

"End her!" he ordered his troops. They didn't comply.

Mortal! The woman ducked and ran against the building, escaping the bullets fired above her head.

Thaddeus listened to a Devil's Wing's chain gun, flipped around, and flew backward. He turned over on the ground, pushed his fists into the sand, and raised up to see an approaching spacecraft that resembled his VTOL. The space vehicle landed ten feet above the ground, and a black-caped figure dropped out of the craft's belly. Her personal legionnaires came down after her and lined up on her flanks.

She lifted from a crouch and walked closer. Her galea and muscle cuirass fit perfectly around her slender body, which was outfitted with tight black spandex. Her black gauntlets and long boots formed a diamond shape midforearm and atop her kneecap. The Crucifier she wielded was that of the dead empress.

Augustine watched her father remove his boot from Codex's body. The legionnaires began to form a circle around her and the emperor. Thaddeus growled at the treacherous soldier. He reached behind his shoulder blades and brought forth the Drakon Venom. He threw it up into a spin and caught it on the descent. "Like your mother, I will enjoy watching you die."

Augustine and her father ran toward each other.

Clash! Clink! Clash!

Behind the emperor, Bryana helped Codex up. They broke through the human wall.

Augustine swept her upper body under the blade and swung the Crucifier at a forty-five-degree angle. The swords collided once more. She used her strength to force his weapon down and kicked him in the chest.

The Tartarus's stone walls crumbled, and he fell face forward. She reached out her hand, lifted him into the air, and threw him through the prison. She sky jumped onto the roof and immediately bounced over the building.

Thaddeus rolled, and her sword slit into the sand. His iron knuckles struck her chin, propelling her into the air. She flipped backward and landed on a knee.

Her chest became heavy. Her hands boiled. Her eyes were aflame. The Crucifier doused in fire, she pointed the lit sword at him.

Thaddeus's Drakon Venom shot lightning at the rushing fire.

Each step forward seemed like one back. Her boots' heels shoveled the sand. Electric shocks surged over her skin. The weapon's force pushed her up and onto her spine.

"You see, I am power incarnate. The master of this universe and the next. The Roman Empire will rise through the flames of the fallen." She stood on both feet to see her father stepping toward her. "Lay down your sword and die a slow death. Continue, and you will pray to me that you had."

Augustine closed her eyes, lowered her head, and relaxed her breathing. Her pupils constricted. The darkness had returned. She opened her eyes at Thaddeus, who had stopped feet away. He nodded.

Do not fail us, said her father.

The dark empress shut her eyes as he dashed her way. She blocked his sword with hers and punched her fist into his chest. She withdrew it from the open cavity and witnessed her father's skin transform to black. He dropped his sword, and his liquid form soon puddled at her feet.

Augustine draped her long cape over her body. She and her soldiers marched toward the main temple.

Soon she ascended the temple's steps and stood before a rectangular altar as her soldiers waited outside. She inhaled and sensed the dark matter that hid the GodSphere below. She held out her hands, and the altar started to crack and crumble. A green orb ascended from below the altar and shattered it in half. Augustine removed her gauntlets and guided the GodSphere between her hands.

"I can't let you do this," said Codex, who was crouched behind a sacrificial table. He pointed the Dr'og rifle at her. "I saw what your father planned to do. Now that he's dead, we can put a stop to this."

She dug her nails into the sphere, turning it black. The orb vibrated and exploded a green light that disappeared, leaving behind green dust particles.

"You have abandoned the empire. Let this be the last time we meet, Legionnaire." She showed her back to Codex and walked out of the temple.

Heads Will Roll

Themis, Planet Boreas—899 CD

The loinclothed men who guarded Themis's entrance simultaneously faced away and clashed their spears' ends on the ground. One grabbed the door's handle and held it open for the empress and her armed legionnaires.

She entered the elders' forbidden domain. Her soldiers formed two lines at her sides as she continued to the center.

"So it is prophesied that you will not kneel before us," an elder said in the open. Augustine saw three hooded bodies come out from separate Roman-arched passageways.

"Our time has arrived." They stopped and knelt by her side. "Let no world learn of this power. Conquer them all. Rome is yours, my empress."

The Crucifier cut their heads clean off in one slice.

Author Biograpgy

When he's not playing his guitar, immersed in writing, or lifting weights at the gym, Rommell C. Lewis is attending graduate school, where he is majoring in management with a concentration in leadership. He is a US Air Force veteran who has proudly served his country for fifteen years in the United States and abroad. The Illinois native also enjoys listening to old-school black, death, and thrash metal.